WINDSWEPT WHISPERS

A CONTEMPORARY ROMANCE STORY

DAWN BACA

To my husband Jeremy,

My very own romance character.

Your love and support has always been the foundation of everything I do.

To Donna, my forever friend,

More than two decades ago, your laughter first brightened my world. Who knew that moment would spark a friendship so enduring? Through the years, your joy, humor, and kindness have been a constant, and I'm so grateful we're still laughing together after all this time.

My love for you is deeper than the oceans and higher than the mountains.

— *Anonymous*

CHAPTER 1
OLIVIA

Wow... I can't believe I used to look up to this woman!!!

It's always the cute ones.

UNFOLLOWED!

I always knew she was a mean girl, lol... NO ONE is that nice.

Such a shame. I wonder what her mother would think of her now...

Three hours ago, before she had landed in Santorini, Olivia had thought it would be a good idea to load her comments section. Now, as she read the comments that had come in about her, knowing what people were saying about her and her family, she couldn't remember why she thought it was a good idea to do so. It was even worse with the gossip column articles she'd downloaded.

But, like a train wreck, she couldn't look away, scrolling through the *endless* comments that had flooded her page and absorbing every single one of them. Each one cut deeper than the last, especially when they talked about how disappointed her mother would be in her. And yet, she couldn't fault them.

She had acted way out of character *that* night— hurt so many people and said such mean things.

No, she deserved every vile comment thrown at her. She deserved every article and meme made of her. She deserved it all and took it like the big girl she knew she was.

It was only once her comments stopped loading that she'd been reminded where she was.

She truly was a coward, as the people online said. Because if she wasn't, she wouldn't have been hiding away in an isolated hotel somewhere in Santorini, with no internet connection and walls so high it felt like the rest of the island didn't exist.

Yes, she was a big, *big* coward. So, she subjected herself to the comments once again, letting each one settle inside of her, serving as punishment she knew she deserved for what she had done.

It had been two weeks already. Two weeks of constant hounding by the public and the paparazzi. Two weeks since she had last known peace. The constant scrutiny had taken such a mental toll on her she was paranoid about the littlest things. Every notification on her phone almost felt like a threat and every time it vibrated, her heart skipped a beat so hard her chest hurt.

Her usually vibrant outlook on life had slowly dimmed with every ping she received on her phone and for every phone call that went unanswered by her best friend. Her hair, usually a vibrant and fiery red mane of bouncy curls, was looking less bouncy and more flat—the red no longer its usual show-stopping asset on her. Her smile had completely vanished. She could barely master the art of moving her lips in the upper direction that curved into a smile, as they seemed to be permanently downturned.

Zayn and Jax were practically involved in a scandal every two to three business days. Is this what it was like for them? Not for the first time, Olivia had wondered.

Her brothers had made such an infamous reputation for themselves that people worried when they didn't hear about a recent scandal they were involved in.

There was no way they were intentionally involved in scandals if this is how it felt to be front and center in one.

Her mind swirled until it became too much. Unable to stand the silence surrounding her and the stiffness of a rarely used room, Olivia pushed up off her feet and explored the place she'd call her home for the foreseeable future.

The hotel room she'd been rushed to when she arrived on the hotel grounds stood isolated from the rest of the hotel. Well, it was more like a cozy flat than a room, with three bedrooms and an entertainment area on the top floor—which contained a beautiful assortment of musical instruments, along with a kitchen, a sitting room, and a dining room on the ground floor.

She was used to the sterile feeling of beige places that looked like they were a set for an interior design catalog than a house one lived in. Heck, even her own bedroom at *her* house lacked the warmth one would expect from such a room, with every piece of furniture staged and meticulously placed to give off the rich vibe her father was very particular about in their white and gold accented mansion.

Here, everything was colorful and cheerful, each room inviting you to stay and take it in with the vibrant colors and furniture made for sitting and not as decoration. By far, the best place had been her bedroom. It was much smaller than what she was used to, and yet, it was the best. What had drawn her to the room, though, were the floor-to-ceiling windows that overlooked a little piece of private beach on their already private beach property.

It was a shame though. All this beauty surrounded her and she couldn't even appreciate it, as restlessness ate away at her bones.

It was the same type of restlessness that drew her back into the bedroom she'd been in just a few minutes ago as she frantically searched for where she had last left her phone. As soon as she found the tiny device, she logged into her phone and refreshed the page to check for new comments, only for the no signal bar to remind her she was truly disconnected from the outside world.

In a fit of anger, which even surprised her with its suddenness, Oliva threw her phone across the room. The sound of her phone pronounced the echo of her enraged scream hitting the wall in a loud thud before it bounced back and ended on the floor, face down. She didn't have any illusions that it had survived the crash. She'd heard the screen crack, which is perhaps why she didn't feel any remorse when she stomped on it.

The crunch that followed offered only a tiny sense of satisfaction that slipped away from her as soon as she'd had it, just like water slipping through one's fingers. And then, she did it again and, once again, the satisfaction was fleeting. She didn't stop until nothing but shards of a ridiculously expensive phone remained.

It was over an hour later, after playing out numerous scenarios that did nothing to relax her, that Olivia decided she needed to do her favorite self-care routine to find some release from the anxiety that was building. Her nerves were fried, her heart was pounding too heavily from her constant worry that she could *feel* it against her ribcage, and her feet were killing her due to the line she'd practically burned into the carpeted floor.

She didn't have her usual luxuries, of course. Her bath bombs and bath salts were missing, and so was her favorite, wildly expensive—but so worth it—

vanilla candle that gave off the most soothing smell and reminded her of a happier time. But she had to make do with what she had because she *needed* it!

In a bid to drown out the world, she put on a music player that came with the place and immediately, unknown up-tempo Greek music blasted through the speakers. She did not understand a word being said, but that didn't matter because the music was serving its purpose.

In the bathtub, she tried to soak away her troubles and shame, pretending like none of it was happening—she was simply on one of her many trips and just enjoying a foreign land.

It kind of, *sort of*, worked but very briefly. However, that was more relief than she had felt in a minute, and at this point, any kind of relief, no matter how brief, was welcome.

Minutes later, when the water turned too cold for her to relax fully, she stepped out of the bathtub, draped one of the large bath towels around herself, and wrapped another, much smaller, one around her long hair.

Olivia had kind of gotten into the groove of the music and was stepping to it in earnest, feeling the freest she had been in a hot minute. She stepped into the bedroom once again, humming to herself as she rummaged through her bags for her lotion. She then went through the very soothing motions of pampering herself with her twelve-step skincare routine, which, before this, only happened every once in a while.

In the back of her mind, the nagging feeling of her worries beckoned her, but she refused to give in to it. She was determined to stay in this carefree moment right now—and she would, goddammit!

It was when she'd stepped into the kitchen moments later that the nagging feeling became a little too hard to ignore. Every step reminded her of everything she had read about herself from the public. Every move she made to the music as she tried to act like everything was okay reminded her that everything was, in fact, not okay.

Her hands shook as she reached for where she'd been told the cups were, but she couldn't stop. She couldn't stop humming and bobbing to the beat of the now muffled music, trying to pretend she had it all together. She moved toward the kitchen pot with the coffee that, thankfully, someone had brewed for her.

"Hello?" a deep voice unexpectedly came from behind her, slicing through the silence that hid behind the loud music.

Olivia let out a loud gasp at the unexpected presence in her private residence as she quickly swung around, the cup she'd been clasping slipping from her shaking hands and unintentionally hurtling toward the intruder.

CHAPTER 2
NIKOS

Nikos had just enough time to sidestep before the ceramic cup collided with his head. The sound of it flying over him was less startling than the warm liquid from the cup splattering all over his body.

Before he could orient himself, the lady in front of him started speaking. "I... uh, sorry, do I know you?" she stammered, acting like she didn't just almost hit him with a freaking cup. And before he could respond, she huffed and stood straight up, her head held high in that haughty way he was so used to with rich girls as she stared down at him. It was quite a sight, seeing as he was many inches taller than she was. "You're my bodyguard, aren't you?" the woman sneered. "I told Dad that I didn't need one!" She glared at him like he had anything to do with whatever her issues were.

"I—" he said, attempting to introduce himself.

"Well, since you're here, please make sure the security is tight, alright? We wouldn't want someone coming in here and violating my privacy."

It was Nikos' turn to huff. He couldn't decide if he wanted to laugh or kick her out. His *Pappouli* had promised him a quiet and drama-free stay, however, the first thing he encountered was drama—and he had been on the island all of five minutes!

The lady standing before him gave him a confused look, probably because he didn't fall over himself, bending to her will, as she expected, before she stomped away. She'd given him a once over, which he used to from all of his time dealing with high society people.

He watched her walk away, wondering how he was going to survive the one month he had promised to his grandparents when he clearly had an entitled brat living in his personal space.

Nikos looked around his meticulously clean house, a sense of nostalgia washing over him, but he pushed it away just as quickly as it had come. He was here for one thing, and one thing alone. He was going to renovate the hotel so he could sell it to the potential buyer he already had lined up. It would be silly to relive memories of his childhood home that somehow still smelled exactly as he remembered it: something bright and fresh—his *yayioula's* very own cleaning fragrance, which told him that while he wasn't living here anymore, his house had been far from abandoned.

Nikos turned around to pick up the suitcase he'd left on the door, only to be greeted by a stained wall where the rest of the liquid had landed. Something about the dull brown stain on his white walls bothered him and brought forward his need to renovate and make sure everything was in pristine order. Unfortunately, if he cleaned up the bothersome stain, he knew he'd barely have finished that before the next stain caught his eye, and he *really* needed to see his grandparents.

He had been talking to them every day since he left over twelve years ago, when he was a teenager. Occasionally, they met off the island and he went on vacation with them. But something about seeing his grandparents again and actually being at home had him too giddy to focus on much else besides reuniting with family.

With his mind made up, Nikos dropped his bag on the table that sat next to the entrance, skipped over the cup on the floor, which thankfully didn't break when it landed on the carpeted floor, and headed to the side of the resort where management resided. He knew he'd find his *papous* there and, hopefully, someone who would clean up the mess.

"Why did you have to rent out *my* place?" was the first thing he said to his *papous* as soon as he found the man. He was exactly where Nikos had thought he'd be—in his office, hunched over mountains of paperwork.

"Nikos, my boy!" the older Kappellis cheered as he brightly smiled at his grandson. "Come here, let me see you." He put out his hands and Nikos walked over to him, leaning down so he was eye-level with his grandfather. "You are a big boy now," his *papous* said in Greek, his smile getting even bigger as if Nikos' presence was the best gift he ever received.

No matter how many times this happened, Nikos would never tire of how his grandparents always acted like they hadn't seen or heard from him in a very long time.

"You say that all the time, *Papou*." Nikos tried to scowl, but he could barely master a frown. His face split in a wide smile as he took a seat in front of his grandfather after they were done with their greetings. He ignored the disapproving look his *papous* sent his way, knowing how much he disliked the fact that Nikos being away for so long made him forget his mother tongue to some extent. "But, seriously," he sighed, not wanting to get started with the topic of preserving the language, culture, and whatnot. "Why my place? We have so many vacant rooms—"

His *papous* gave him *that* look, the same one that always made Nikos reconsider his words. He sat straighter in his seat, trying to act like the subtle glare and raised eyebrow did not affect him anymore. But, of course, it did. The second his grandfather had *the* look, Nikos knew he was headed toward trouble and should carefully reconsider what he was saying and *how* he was saying it.

"You have heard of Xander Clarke, yes?" *Papous* said after making sure the base in Nikos' voice dropped.

No matter how old he got, Nikos would always find the older Kappellis a very intimidating man.

"Vaguely," Nikos replied in a neutral tone, suppressing his irritation so it didn't come through. He knew that his family had been working with generations of Clarkes as long as they'd had the hotel. He just wasn't sure which one was Xander because he had been very disconnected from the family business.

"That's his daughter, Olivia, and she needs our help for as long as she wants it."

"Help with what?" *And* why should *we* have to help her? Of course, he didn't say this out loud. He didn't have a death wish.

"That's not really our business," *Papous* said as he shuffled some papers around him. "*Our* business," he leveled Nikos with a look, "is me knowing when you want to take over so I can fully retire."

And there it was... The one topic Nikos did *not* want to get into. One he'd *hoped* he would avoid, at least for a few days.

"I—I, uhhh..." he stammered as he looked around for an excuse, anything to change this topic. He shifted uncomfortably in the chair he sat in, the weight of his *papous'* expectant stare weighing him down.

For the longest time, Nikos had known that his family expected for him to be the one to take over management of the hotel so his grandparents could enjoy their final years. It had never been much of a problem until he left the island and had aspirations of his own. Coming back and setting up a life here had been something that he absolutely dreaded.

That his *papous* took his coming to visit as a sign that he was ready to take over just brought home the full weight of these expectations.

His grandfather's expectant stare didn't waiver, patiently waiting for him to answer. Nikos felt exposed, almost vulnerable, as the words threatened to spill out that he would *ne*ver take over the management of the hotel.

"I'm thrilled that you have come back to work with us full-time," *Papous* said, as if in encouragement, except he might as well have just shoved a dagger through Nikos' heart. "Your *yioula* is excited too," he added, twisting the metaphorical dagger even deeper into Nikos' chest. Adding *Yiayia* to the mix reminded Nikos of just how much he was going to disappoint his grandparents. "We can finally step away from the family business, knowing it's now in excellent hands," *Papous* piled on even more, unaware of the turmoil his words awakened in his grandson.

"Yeah," Nikos laughed awkwardly as he adjusted his collar, not knowing how he could even branch the subject of him not wanting to take over now that *Papous* had expressed his feelings about retirement.

And why was it too hot in the room, for Christ's sake?

Before coming to the island, he'd rehearsed this

very scenario multiple times. He knew what he wanted to say when this very subject came up, and he'd hoped he'd simply blurt out his true feelings and intentions.

I don't want to run the hotel but, don't worry, I already have a buyer lined up, is what he thought he'd say. Except he didn't count on the other side of the conversation. The one where he'd have to look into his *papous'* eyes and tell him that the legacy he had talked about over and over all Nikos' life—the one where they passed the hotel to the next generation to run it as generations before they had—was actually going to end with him. And, even worse, that Nikos had no intention of upholding said legacy.

He especially hadn't anticipated the hopeful look his *papous* would wear as he tried to sell the idea of Nikos now owning the hotel like it was the best thing that would ever happen to him. The bitter taste in his mouth didn't leave him as his grandfather moved on to discussing his unexpected roommate, as he gave him rules on how to live with the girl.

They both ignored the fact that Nikos never gave him an official answer—or at least, it looked like *Papous* did. The unspoken words and unanswered questions echoed a little too loudly in his brain.

CHAPTER 3
OLIVIA

Dinner, Oliva had been told, was a communal affair after she requested it brought to her room. It was part of the hotel's initiative of connecting while disconnecting or some similar bullshit the busboy had fed her while roaming the grounds just in front of her isolated accommodation.

And, now, here she was, walking down the never ending maze of hallways that took her outside and back inside repeatedly. She got lost as soon as she left the private compound of her accommodations, but she found she didn't care very much. Eventually, she would find her way to where she needed to go or, at least, find someone who could direct her to where she needed to go.

Her bodyguard had made himself scarce, and she half hoped that it was because he had actually left. While she would like the company of someone to keep her sane, even if they didn't talk much, it was easier to have her meltdowns without an audience. Like the one she had a few minutes before she decided she needed food. *That* had been all shades of ugly as she screamed into her pillow, cried, and then screamed some more.

Maybe it was her continued string of bad luck that was mocking her, because as soon as she came to the conclusion that the benefits of being without company outweighed those of being with them, the man from earlier rounded the corner, coming down the same hall she was meandering.

She let out a disappointed sigh before she put on her best rich-girl attitude—the forced public persona, thanks to who her family was and the people she kept around her. "Take me to the dining hall," she said to him without preamble.

The man, startled by her presence, looked at her funny, his expression being completely obvious as he stood a few feet away from her.

"I said," she glared, adding a little bite in her tone, "do your job and take me to the dining hall."

He had been looking at the floor as he walked,

lost in thought, so Olivia knew he probably didn't hear her and her attitude was uncalled for. However, she could barely muster the energy to be her usual calm and collected self around people, the memory of her most recent mistake so raw it bled. So, instead, she adopted the one persona that never failed to get her what she wanted.

The man glared at her, conflicted with himself as his dark eyes swarmed with a lot of emotion. However, as soon as she'd noticed, they cleared and his face was a mask of indifference. "Right this way," he stated as he turned and walked back to where he had come from, not waiting or looking back to see if Olivia was following him.

In another life, Olivia would have found him beautiful and just the kind of man she was usually attracted to. He was taller than her 5'4" self and the actual definition of tall, dark, and handsome. He was lean, like he kept himself in shape, but didn't spend most of his time working out. He had an angular jawline that people paid good money to attain, a sharp nose that gave him a haughty look, and slightly thin but pink lips accentuated by a short beard. He kept his hair long, and she had the strangest desire to run her fingers through it, especially the edges that slightly curled out as if they had intentionally been styled that way.

In another life, she would have loved to get to know if he liked having his hair pulled and exactly how hard. But the thought of opening up and letting someone in like *that* so soon made her stomach turn.

It was minutes later when Olivia paid attention to her surroundings. It had to have been the lack of noise in a moderately noisy hotel, or maybe it was the feeling of being watched that jarred her out of her thoughts and back to her surroundings.

For the first time since she arrived, she realized exactly how many people were living at this hotel, and it seemed like over a hundred people had all stopped to look at her. She tried to ignore the stares in the long room, hoping and praying to the heavens that there was someone else behind her who they were all looking at. She even subtly turned around to make sure, but she was greeted by the outside and the distant sound of the sea in the evenings.

And, once she did that, she couldn't ignore the fact that the finger-pointing and whispering were being made toward her. Attempting to push through the discomfort, Olivia pressed forward, but the prying eyes and probing questions of the other guests unnerved her to a point where she just couldn't take one more step inside the large room that now felt *very* small.

A few steps away from her, Nikos walked on, oblivious to what was going on around him or the woman he was being forced to be civil with. The only reason he even agreed to walk her to the dining area was that he felt he had already disappointed *Papous*. There was no reason to add to that disappointment, even if the elderly man didn't know it already. So, he swallowed his pride and entertained the spoiled princess, acting as her personal guide, even if he could have asked, literally, anyone else to do it instead.

It's because Nikos was so consumed with his thoughts and shame about his earlier conversation with *Papous* that he missed the fact that the woman he had been leading to the dining hall was now making a hasty retreat behind him. Or the fact that a few people sent greetings his way that he didn't hear.

"What did you want to—" He stopped just as quickly when he eventually turned around to find that the woman he thought was behind him wasn't there anymore.

Had he been walking too fast for her to keep up?

Why didn't she say so? And now he has to go out and look for her? As if this day wasn't already exhausting.

"The poor dear," he heard someone say at the table a few feet away from him.

That's when he noticed that everyone's attention was seemingly taken by something outside the dining hall door. "What's going on?" he asked the first person he saw. It was a drop-dead gorgeous blonde, green-eyed woman who'd made her way to the long food table next to him as she eyed him up and down like she wanted to eat him.

"Olivia Clarke is here," the woman scoffed, almost in disdain. "Can you believe her? After what she did?"

"What?" Nikos asked, confused as he looked around like answers would jump out of thin air to fill in the gaps of what he was missing.

Olivia Clarke was the woman he had promised his *papous* he would look after and the one who seemed to think he was her bodyguard. He didn't care to know much about her beyond those two facts, and yet, the way this woman glared at the empty space where Olivia should have been had his interest officially peaked.

What was her story?

"That little Clarke darling," the woman sneered, "showing her face in public and walking around like she isn't the snake we've always suspected her to be."

"Darling, let's not disturb our host," a wrinkly old man interrupted the woman as he put a hand around her in a manner of possession that was, quite frankly, not warranted.

The last thing on Nikos' mind was showing any interest in a woman, especially this one whose words about Olivia rubbed him the wrong way for some reason. He just wanted to be away from her presence now, pretty much the same way the woman wanted to be away from the old man's presence—if her flinching when he touched her was anything to go by.

"If you'll excuse me," he rushed out, wanting to leave before they did things that would give him nightmares for days. The man's hand had been much lower on her back than what's considered polite in public. Nikos' suspicions about Olivia's whereabouts were confirmed when he got to his house and heard her stomping around the upper stairs. "Food will be here soon," he said as he entered her room. Naturally, he would have knocked first, but the door was wide open and he could see her back as she hunched over something on the bed.

"No thanks," she said distractedly, then rushed out of sight. Nikos moved further into the room, driven by the need to know if she was doing okay. "I'm leaving," she announced as she got back into the room, a bag in hand.

"Why?" he asked, taken aback.

Now that he was fully in the room, he could see her bags and everything thrown around haphazardly.

"I just... I *can't* stay here," she said, throwing the smaller bag into the large suitcase on her bed and then rushing away once again.

"Why not?" He tried to press when she came back to the room, but she didn't respond. She just shook her head like she didn't want to have this conversation. "Okay, could you at least eat first?" he asked, choosing not to pursue whatever was going on with her. Besides, if she left, then he won't have to do whatever she wanted the way his *papous* wanted him to. "My *papous* would kill me if I let you leave without feeding you."

"Your *papous*?" She looked up at him, confused, while still hunched around the overflowing suitcase she was trying to close.

"My grandfather," he elaborated.

"I get that!" she said with a little agitation,

"What I don't get is why your *papous* would care if I ate food or not."

The doorbell rang downstairs, alerting him of the arrival of their food.

"My *papous* owns this place," he said nonchalantly. "You are his guest, so, of course, he would care if you ate or not."

He missed seeing the look of shock Olivia shot his way as he moved to go receive their food.

CHAPTER 4
OLIVIA

The midnight moon hung in the sky, casting a silver glow over the private part of the hotel. Olivia sat close to the beach, curled in on herself, as she absentmindedly watched the waves hit the shore and then rolled back over and over in an almost hypnotic way.

The chilly night air bit into her skin in a way that was almost painful, but she barely noticed. Today officially marked exactly three weeks since the scandal and also the longest she had ever gone without speaking to her confidant and best friend, Ava.

It hurt.

It hurt so badly to think that she didn't have that anymore, especially because she had tried to reach out, even when she knew it was useless. They'd always joked about the fact that nothing could separate them and had gone through literal hell together, only to end up here, with one friend's betrayal hanging between them.

What sucked the most is that this is the kind of thing she would spend hours talking to Ava about until the heaviness in her heart had lessened. This reminder only served to keep her in a loop of sadness and bad reminders until it felt like the tears she had been holding at bay for so long were choking her now. The only comfort she found was with the tiny pendant around her neck that she played with. It was a necklace that used to belong to her mother and held a picture of the two of them.

Olivia remembered the days when she was a child and would run to her mother for anything. Her mother used to hold her and walk her through whatever she was facing, effortlessly making everything better. Now, as an adult who was facing, quite literally, the hardest thing she ever had to go through, she wished upon everything holy that her mother was there to hold her and tell her that everything would be okay.

And yet, the pendant was a reminder that she wasn't there anymore. It especially reminded her how disappointed her mother would be in the person she had become and the choices she had made that brought her here now. And it was with that reminder that Olivia finally broke down. The heaviness in her heart multiplied tenfold when she thought of how disappointed her mother would be in her.

Her pain-filled sobs carried into the night, as she curled in on herself even tighter, feeling the fight drain out of her with how long she had tried to be strong.

If her father was there, he would tell her to suck it up and hold her head high. He'd remind her she was a Clarke and "Clarkes don't show their weakness ever." That's what he'd been saying to her since the scandal.

Once again, the reminder of the reality of her life made her miss her mother because *she* would have understood. She wouldn't tell Olivia to suck it up. Instead, she'd hold her as she cried and then help her fix her mistakes. According to her father, she should ignore it all until it went away.

Olivia pulled her legs even further into her body, attempting to seek comfort where there was none and sinking into the misery of her loneliness. She let out all the humiliation she'd felt since she woke up and realized her face was all over the news. She let out the pain and panic that had driven her to seek out Ava, only to be shut out, and she especially let out the helplessness she couldn't ignore, as it felt like control of her life slipped away.

A LOT of things had bothered Nikos since he got home. The unfamiliarity of his childhood home, that he kept meeting people he didn't know who seemed to know everything about him—courtesy of his grandparents, of course—and the fact that he was sharing his living space with a stranger. But, perhaps, more than anything, it was the fact that he was lying to his *papous*, who for all he knew, Nikos was back to take over the family business.

His grandparents had asked him time and again to come home and he always said he had something to do, but now that he was here, of course, they thought he was back for good. What had once been a sanctuary now felt like a place of torture, as the quietness in his house did nothing to silence his running thoughts.

Back in New York, he never had to focus on his thoughts because the sounds of an active city helped drown them out more often than not. And now, that was all he could focus on.

The door to the balcony of his room was wide open. The biting night air reached him from his double bed and yet he felt hot, uncomfortably so. There was something about not being honest with his grandparents that just didn't sit right with him. He wasn't even lying at all. He just wasn't telling the truth, but that still felt like lying.

Nikos tried to think of what he could do to make it better because telling the truth about his intentions was out of the question. *Maybe if I fall asleep, I'll wake up feeling better*, he thought.

The more Nikos thought about it, the more it made sense, so he threw the blanket that was wrapped around his torso off and jumped out of bed. He was too worked up to fall asleep, so he needed to at least relax, and he knew just the place he should go.

The beach had a calming effect that the more he thought about it, the more he realized just how much he had missed being here. When he was a child, his father would take him out there and they'd just sit around, listening to the waves—something that his mother didn't like. She would fuss over him, wanting them both to cover up and come back inside after only a few minutes. And yet, every night, his father would take him back out and they'd just sit around. Or, at least, his father sat around.

Nikos was the typical child who could not stay still for more than a few minutes. Sometimes, his grandparents joined them too, but more often than not, it was just him and his dad.

It had taken him a long time to go back to the beach after he lost his parents because all it had done was remind him that his father wasn't with him anymore. But he'd worked up the courage before he left the island altogether. Now, as he made his way toward the beach, shoes in hand, he looked forward to connecting with the feeling that always settled over him when he was by the water.

However, before he made it to the spot where the sea met the sand on his private side of the hotel, he heard the sounds of silent sobs. Stopping for a second, right before his feet hit the white sand, Nikos looked around for where the sounds were coming from. Just a short distance ahead of him, he saw a woman sitting right by the spot where the after met the sand, shoulders shaking as she curled up into the fetal position.

He wanted to take a step and check on her, but she let out another wail that was so gut wrenching that it stopped him in his tracks. Nikos looked around, checking to see if anyone else was around before he remembered this part of the beach was closed off from the public. *So, the crying woman had to be his roommate, right?*

It made sense given the shiny red hair, but she confirmed her identity when she lifted her head, looked around like she remembered she was not in the privacy of her own home, and then broke down once again.

Ever since he met her, he had brushed her off as a spoiled princess who was used to getting everything she wanted. She even walked around like she was untouchable, and yet, right now, she looked anything but untouchable. He debated if he should check on her but, ultimately, walked to a different area of the beach to tire himself out.

WHEN HE WALKED into the kitchen the next day, he was surprised to find her already sitting there so early in the morning. He was certain he had gone to bed before her. He would never admit it, but he'd ended up checking on her once again before he went to bed.

"Good morning," she said, startling him.

"Good morning," Nikos echoed, looking at her suspiciously.

"I made coffee. You want some?" she followed up as she got up from the kitchen stool.

"I got it," he said, stopping her from pouring him a cup, and made his way toward the counter. This is the longest she has gone without being haughty and he was officially suspicious.

"I never got your name," he heard her say behind him as he fidgeted with the cups.

"Nikos," he answered after an extended pause.

When she didn't follow up with another question or statement, he finally turned and looked at her, *really* taking her in.

She looked... tired. Heavy shadows hung under her eyes and her red mane of hair looked like she'd run a hand through it one too many times.

"Nice to meet you," she whispered as she ducked her head and arranged her hair so it fell into her face, hiding her face from him.

CHAPTER 5
OLIVIA

L ast night, when Olivia found out that the man she had thought was her bodyguard actually owned the hotel, her embarrassment had not allowed her to stay in his presence for longer than it took her to say, "Oh."

But, after her long and draining but strangely rejuvenating cry at the beach, she decided she needed to get her life in order and stop with the pity party. She made the conscious decision to stop running from her problems, and that started with making amends with her host, who she'd definitely insulted with her assumptions. However, the unnerving way he looked at her made it impossible to actually face him and apologize. She felt his sharp eyes penetrate the barrier that her long hair usually provided when she needed it.

Yesterday, he'd looked at her like she was a pest, bothering his existence, though he never outright came out and said it. And, maybe, it made sense that he'd been looking at her like that because not only did she treat him like the help at *his* hotel, but she'd also acted like the spoiled rich brat everyone thought she was.

But now... now he looked at her with *that* look. The one people usually got when they realized her glamorous life wasn't as amazing as it looked, where they looked like they pitied her.

She hated it. She hated it so, *so* much that her fingers wrapped around her coffee mug a little too tightly as she fought the urge to curse him out. The look was one that always made her feel small and as though someone was opening her up and dissecting every piece of her. Usually, it was followed by the very condescending "Oh... honey."

If he says it, I will punch him, Olivia thought.

"Can I help you?" she blurted out, unable to take the scrutiny.

Nikos made a noise but said nothing as he busied himself with whatever. "Glad to see you didn't run away last night," he said eventually, and then he slid a plate of fruits right in her line of sight.

"I didn't have anywhere else to go," she admitted, but immediately wanted to take it back because that was very pathetic of her to admit. "I mean... I—I didn't have anywhere to go because I don't have any cash on me and I lost my phone," she compensated.

The truth was, she *really* didn't have anywhere to go. She'd come to that realization shortly after her suitcase was fully packed and she'd reached for her phone, only to find that it wasn't where she usually kept it in her back pocket.

"So, Nikos," she rushed out, not wanting to dwell on the embarrassment that was heating her cheeks. "What's there to do around here?" She tried to sound casual, hoping to shift the focus away from the earlier awkwardness.

Thankfully, Nikos took the bait. "There's plenty to do here. It really just depends on what you are into."

"Oh yeah? Like what?"

She risked a peek at him to find Nikos looking at her, only he looked with great intensity and, definitely, no pity. That had a strangely calming effect on her as she felt her shoulders relax and the grip on her mug loosening immensely. It didn't look like he was entertaining her out of pity, which was the best she could hope for.

"Well, we have a spa, a sauna, and all that pampering stuff, if that's the kind of day you are looking for. But, outside the walls of the hotel, you can check out a lot of local cafes, historical sites, the beach..."

"Sounds nice." Olivia managed a weak smile, but held back the words she really wanted to say.

She was looking for something that would take her away from crowds and not toward them. Nothing Nikos said sounded appealing. Thankfully, she was saved from making any more conversation when Nikos' phone alarm went off.

Deciding now was as good a time as any to excuse herself, Olivia tied her hair in a bun to get it out of the way and stood up from her chair, her cup in hand but the untouched fruit plate left where it was in case Nikos was going to eat the fruits.

"Uh... Olivia?" Nikos called from where he stood.

"Yeah?" she responded absentmindedly as she washed out her cup and then bent over to place it in the dishwasher.

"You... huhmm..."

Confused by his sudden change in attitude, Olivia turned around only to find Nikos giving her an intense look once again. Except, this time, it held something darker as he scanned her from head to toe and back. Too late, Olivia realized that her hair had been the shield covering the goods since her very thin nightie did nothing to hide anything.

In her rush to pack up, she had only packed one piece of night clothing and it was this black number that Ava had bought her as a prank, but it had somehow ended up being her favorite thing. It was this little thing made of mesh and strategically placed flowers around her chest area and between her legs, but otherwise, everything else was on display. And by everything, it meant *everything*— and she had bent over just a second ago.

"Oh god!" Olivia exclaimed as she covered herself with her hands. "Sorry, I didn't mean to... I mean, I didn't realize," she stammered, feeling her cheeks grow warm. She quickly undid her hair from the bun and let it fall over her once again.

Dear heavens! Why her? Why?

"Here," Nikos said as he took off his jacket, then quickly draped it over her.

"Thank you," Olivia whispered, pulling it around herself like it was a shield.

"I should get going," Nikos said. He pulled the

plate of fruit from where it was and headed to the fridge.

"Where are you going?" Olivia asked as she didn't want to sit in the awkwardness that silence would bring, and yet, she regretted it immediately. Making extra conversation meant that it would take Nikos and the embarrassment that had befallen her that much longer to go away.

"I need to meet my *Yiayia* and *Papous*," he responded, which she didn't think he would. But this reminded her of her blunder from yesterday and how she had acted toward him with her assumptions.

"Why didn't you correct me earlier? When I, you know, mistook you for someone else?" She asked him, grateful for the chance to apologize and carry one less burden.

Nikos, now standing by the sink right next to her, turned to face her. "Would it have made a difference?" he questioned, his tone almost challenging.

"I don't know," she admitted after a beat. "But, I am sorry. The woman from yesterday, that's not me. I'm usually not so..."

"Callous?" he supplemented when she trailed off.

"Something like that," Olivia sighed as she looked away from him.

"Hey," Nikos said, and then unexpectedly, he held her chin and tilted her head so she was looking up at him. The simple move shot a zing of electricity throughout her body, making her let out a silent gasp. Nikos didn't let go of her face and held eye contact with her like he was trying to communicate something to her.

"It's all good, Olivia," he whispered, like they were sharing a secret.

And, maybe, she was overthinking the simple gesture, but it oddly felt like his eyes were tracing every inch of her face.

Olivia realized Nikos was now so close to her that his breath caressed her face when he spoke. His spicy cologne that lingered on his jacket had multiplied tenfold as the man stood impossibly close to her.

Her heart pounded loudly in her chest, throat dry, and hands clammy as, for the briefest of seconds, she thought about throwing caution to the wind and doing something very, *very* stupid. And yet Nikos' intense and serious stare thankfully held her back.

"I don't remember giving you my name," Olivia

whispered back, her eyes briefly shooting to his lips and then back to his intense eyes.

Would they be as soft as they look? Would I be so reckless as to find out?

"I own this place. I know the names of everyone who is staying here."

His face broke out in the briefest of smiles and she knew, then and there, that whatever had transpired in the past few seconds was gone. Thankfully, too, because she didn't know what had overcome her when he was holding her face. They both took a step back from each other at the same time, breaking the spell completely.

"I have to go," Olivia said.

"I have to go," Nikos echoed at the same time.

He let out an amused laugh while Olivia shifted from one foot to the other, eyes darting everywhere but at him as she looked for an escape.

Thankfully, Nikos gave her one. "Goodbye, Olivia. Enjoy the rest of your day."

Then, she watched as he left, leaving her alone with the thoughts of what the hell just happened as she tried to tamper down the fluttering in her stomach caused by the way her name rolled off his tongue.

CHAPTER 6
NIKOS

Nikos used to play a little game when he was a young boy. He would close his eyes and count how many steps it took him from one place of the hotel to the next. His favorite path had always been finding his way to his grandparents' house. From his family's home, it would be eighty-five steps. If he was coming from the office, it would take him twenty-five steps. From the main entrance to the hotel grounds, it would take him two-hundred-twenty-five steps.

This was something that had always brought him so much joy and had helped him map out the hotel. He could move around it with his eyes closed. The memories of him running into walls and having his father or mother correct his steps as he moved around with closed eyes echoed in the halls as he made his way to his *Papous* and *Yiayia*. But he had gone a long time without allowing those memories out, and he wasn't about to do so now.

So, instead of focusing on a spot where he once hit his toes as he mapped out the hotel, he focused on how the paint looked chipped and would need to be fixed before he could take the needed pictures of the hotel. He refused to acknowledge the flowers climbing the ledges as a memory of his mother's effort to "add personality" to their hotel and instead focused on how they needed to be trimmed and tamed for a more professional look. And, on and on he went, trying to replace the memories he didn't know he still held with ideas of work and things that needed to be fixed.

By the time he made it to his destination on the other side of the hotel grounds, he had a whole list of tasks he needed to do and not enough time to be nostalgic. *It was perfect.* Ironically, the nostalgia he was running from jumped out at him as soon as he entered his grandparents' house. Even before he had entered the house, he had already smelled the food cooking and he could only imagine how much his *Yiayia* had cooked for them.

He found both of his grandparents in the homey,

brightly colored kitchen, his *Yiayia* bent over a large pot on the stove while his *Papous* arranged dishes overflowing with food on the counter that sat in the middle of the kitchen.

"Are you expecting company?" Nikos said, his eyes scanning the dishes.

"Nikos, *mou*!" *Yiayia* exclaimed when they both turned around to see him. "Come here," she beckoned, hands outstretched.

She looked just the same as Nikos remembered from the last time he saw her. Her white hair pulled back in a bun, a cloth over it. She wore her favorite black dress with the frilly pink apron *Papous* had bought her as a present a long time ago. Her face had more smile lines than age lines and her brown eyes were looking at him as warmly as she'd always been.

"*Yiayia*," Nikos' smile stretched wide, matching his grandmother's as he fell into her embrace. She smelled just like he remembered—a fresh, fruity smell with a lot of baked goods.

Yiayia was many inches shorter than him, and yet Nikos always felt tiny when she hugged him. It was such a deep reminder of his childhood that the memories he'd been trying to drown out threatened to come back up and remind him of happier times when his parents were still here.

Nikos pulled back, a lump in his throat, and let out a laugh when *Yiayia* took his face and turned it every which way, like she was assessing him for the very first time. Her hands were warm but her fingers were cold, a contrast that was just so... *Yiayia*!

"You've lost weight," she commented as she pulled back. "Are you not eating well?" And before he could answer, she added, "Not to worry, I will fix that." *Yiayia* pointed to a chair next to where *Papous* stood, and Nikos took the seat without question.

No matter how many times he told *Yiayia* that he was taking care of himself and eating well, she always commented on his weight, telling him he looked skinny and needed to eat more. This was usually accompanied by her cooking large amounts of food, like the ones on display all around the kitchen.

After years of teaching him how to cook and take care of himself, you'd think *Yiayia* was content that she taught him enough to live by. But Nikos wasn't complaining. It had been a while since someone cared about him enough to worry about things like his health, so he welcomed it wholeheartedly.

Papous gave him a brief hug and then went

around to where *Yiayia* was cooking, picking up a spatula and dipping it in the cooking pot.

"Get out of my kitchen, Dimitrios!" *Yiayia* shouted at *Papous* in Greek. "Now, I need to wash this again," she mumbled as pulled the spatula from his hands and moved to the sink.

"But you don't *have* to," *Papous* responded as he reached for another spatula, but stopped when *Yiayia* turned to glare at him. He promptly put his hands up and backed away to move back to the other side of the counter, close to Nikos. "Your *Yayioula*," *Papous* shook his head like he was disappointed, and yet the tiny smile he was wearing said otherwise.

This was a familiar dance Nikos realized he had missed. Ever since he could remember, his grandparents always argued about things like this. *Yiayia* was the kind to pick up as she cooked, wanting everything to be clean and in order. *Papous*, on the other hand, preferred cleaning up after the cooking *and* eating were done, something that drove his wife crazy. He also liked to taste everything he cooked so he could adjust the flavor accordingly, whereas *Yiayia* didn't believe in eating food as one cooked.

They never really spent time in the kitchen together because of this, each preferring to let the other do things their way, so Nikos was surprised that they were in the kitchen together now.

"Nikos, how is that girlfriend of yours? What's her name?" *Yiayia* asked as she scrubbed the spatula *Papous* had used.

Nikos quickly shuffled through his memories, trying to remember the last woman he'd introduced to his grandparents. Tammy came to mind. She was a woman he used to have a mutually beneficial friends-with-benefits situation with whom accidentally answered his phone when they called a few months ago.

"Tammy?" he asked tentatively, not sure if that's who *Yiayia* meant.

"Yes! Tammy. How is that sweet child?"

Nikos snorted at the fact that his *Yiayia* thought Tammy was a "sweet girl". That woman was anything but sweet. However, at the risk of getting hit with the spatula in *Yiayia's* hands, he kept that to himself. "She's okay," he responded, "But, we, uh, broke up."

They hadn't, really. She got freaked out because his grandparents wanted to meet her and that was the last time he ever saw her. Not that it had affected him. He knew where they stood when they'd gotten together. However, he wondered what it would be like to have a woman he truly liked meet his *Papous* and *Yiayia*.

"Oh–"

"It's alright," he stopped his *Yiayia* from starting the pity party. "We weren't a good match."

"Good match?" *Papous* scoffed, "Me and your *Yiayia* didn't know each other until the day we got married. But look at us now. Fifty-two years later, and I wouldn't want another woman next to me." *Papous* had that twinkle in his eyes that he always got when he spoke about *Yiayia* and the life they had.

"Love grows, Nikos," *Yiayia* said as she smiled at *Papous*. "You need to be willing to put in the work."

They shared a look so full of love that Nikos had to look away because it felt like he was intruding on a very private moment.

"Times have changed, *Yiayia*," he said, as he reached for a cupcake. "Arranged marriages are not a thing anymore."

Thankfully! If it was, she would have married him off a long time ago.

"Well, they should be," *Yiayia* said, as she swatted his hands from reaching for a second one. "Young people, these days, run away at the first sign of danger, and I will never understand it. Did you know that the Stamopoulos boy is on his fourth wife now? He barely spent a few weeks with the third one."

"Maybe they weren't compatible," Nikos made a throwaway comment as he bit into his muffin. *Vanilla with chocolate swirl. His favorite!*

Christos Stamopoulos was a friend he grew up with and used to know. He was never the type to settle and was always off, looking for the next big thing. Nikos wasn't really surprised that the man treated his relationships the same way.

"Not compatible? What does that even mean? You see your grandfather and me? Are we compatible?" She glared at him like he did something wrong.

Nikos shrugged, not wanting to be at the end of *Yiayia's* wrath.

"When we first met, I didn't like his face," she started.

"Hey!" *Papous* protested. "I'm sitting right here!"

"He smelled weird," she continued, like *Papous* didn't say anything. "I didn't like the way he chewed his food or the way he refused to cook for me. There was a lot to not like, but the more I observed, the more I realized there was much more to him. I doubt the Stamopoulos boy is staying long enough to *look*. Whatever he's chasing with these relationships, he needs to find it within himself."

Maybe you should tell him that. Nikos didn't voice said thoughts, otherwise it might turn into him running errands with her he just could not handle at the moment.

"I hope you are not like that too," she warned, pointing the clean spatula threateningly in his face. "I want to have grandbabies and that won't happen if you can't commit to a relationship."

Great-grandbabies. The correction was at the tip of his tongue, but Nikos swallowed it down.

His grandparents had married young, and so had his parents. When *Yiayia* and *Papous* lost their only son when Nikos was only eight, they took him in and treated him as their own child. I guess it makes sense that they would think of his children as grandbabies and not great-grandbabies. Besides, no one needed that grim reminder right now.

Yiayia then moved on, talking about all the people they knew and what they were up to, which served as the distraction Nikos needed to close his thoughts from the missing family he never got a chance to share his greatest moments with. That was quite the fit though, since his grandparents had numerous photographs scattered all over the house, the kitchen included, and his parents featured in a lot of them.

By the time he was updated on everything he'd missed on the island, they were finished eating and putting the leftovers away. *Yiayia* was working on gift baskets of baked goods she was going to send to a few people, something she always did every time she baked quite a lot.

"Nikos," *Papous* called him, "walk with me." He indicated to the back of the house and didn't wait for Nikos to react before he turned and followed. The look *Papous* was wearing let him know he might not like the conversation they were about to have. "So, have you decided yet when you are ready to move back and run the family business?" *Papous* asked as soon as they hit the beach.

Nikos knew the question was coming, and yet he wasn't prepared. Just knowing that *Papous* was eager to step down filled him with immense shame that he had to look away from the older man and focus on the people he could see parasailing over the sea.

"I believe in you, Nikos," *Papous* said, probably misinterpreting his silence. "You've accomplished so much, and I know you'll succeed in running the business. Your dad would be proud of what you've become." He couldn't decide what was worse. That *Papous* thought he only needed a little encouragement, that he was lying, or that if his father was here and he knew of Nikos' actual plans for the hotel, it would be anything but pride he exuded. After a prolonged silence, *Papous* shifted his approach, as if sensing Nikos' inner struggle. "I hope you'll decide to stay longer with us, my boy. You don't have to make a decision about the hotel now, but your *Yayioula* has missed having you around. I have too."

Although the words sounded anything but, Nikos heard the plea in his *Papous'* voice and he just about lost it. He hadn't cried for any reason in a very long time, but tears were coming to his eyes now, along with the taste of shame bitter on his tongue. Here he was, hoping to sell the hotel, get it off his hands, and move on with the life he had built in America, while his grandparents hoped that he would choose to stay and rebuild a life with them.

For the first time since he got the brilliant idea to sell, Nikos wondered if he was making the right decision after all.

CHAPTER 7
OLIVIA

"I can't believe you, Dad!" Olivia fumed down at the phone in her hands. "You sent me away without contact from the outside world, and now you call only to tell me about some stupid movie?"

"It's not stupid, Olivia!" Xavier Clarke growled on the other end of the line. "It's the next big thing, and your grandfather worked hard to secure you as the lead actress."

"Worked hard" meant he probably intimidated someone into getting her the role. Olivia wasn't new to her family dynamics, especially the way her father twisted words.

"I don't care about the stupid movie!" she screamed in frustration.

Thankfully, the other patrons of the hotel seemed more interested in hanging on the beach than the swimming pool, where she was right now. She couldn't take any more public embarrassment.

"Olivia!" her father shouted loud enough for her to momentarily remove the phone from her ear. "Stop being an entitled brat and be grateful for the chance to be chosen over that Ilyana woman!"

"Grateful?" she scoffed. "Yes, I *should* be grateful that I am a freaking twenty-three-year-old whose father still runs her life."

"You better drop that tone when you're speaking to me," her father said. "And you will take on that movie role and give it your best. You will not disgrace this family."

Of course, in typical Xavier Clarke fashion, he never forgot to remind his children of his expectations of them living up to the family name. God forbid that one of them had a dream that was anything other than being a Hollywood superstar.

"Dad—" she started, dropping the attitude as she hoped to reason with him, but he cut her off.

"I have to go. I'm still dealing with this mess you created." And then she heard the beep of the phone as he hung up.

Olivia let out a frustrated scream, having

nothing else to release all the pent-up anger and frustration a few seconds after speaking to her father built up inside her.

She started acting when she was exactly three weeks old. Her mother was in this one movie where, like her, her TV character had given birth. It caused quite a buzz when people found out that the child in the film was the beloved Gemma Clarke's biological child. She was also the youngest starring actor in her family, as her brothers had started acting when they were at least ten, which meant even more buzz for the movie and the family.

While many people in their circle saw this as a blessing, Olivia looked at it as anything but. Life only grew harder the older she got, as she explored different interests in the limited time she was afforded. For as long as she could remember, there was always the unspoken expectation that she would become just as great of an actress as her mother and live up to the "greatness" of her family. Where her friends had daycare and kindergarten and were busy making friends and memories with children their age, she was on set, looking up at one adult and then another surrounded by cameras. Where they were teenagers making friends and living life as teenagers should, she was in etiquette training and acting classes, with the not-so-subtle reminder of never embarrassing her family thrown in her face every now and again.

She was doomed from the first time she made her movie appearance as a toddler, but even more so when her mother tragically passed away. She was always Gemma Clarke's daughter. But after losing her mother, she became "the next Gemma Clarke" and life had never been the same.

Her father, the one person she thought would be her cheerleader, cared more about the family's reputation and legacy than his own daughter's feelings. So, of course, that did nothing to alleviate the pressure for her to be someone she knew she wasn't. What's worse is that he stopped caring about what his little girl wanted and, instead, started doing what he thought she should want for her.

They didn't listen. Nobody did. And if only she could—

"Miss?" came a voice from behind her, reminding Olivia that she wasn't alone. She whirled around and came face to face with the man who had come from God knows where, a phone in his hand and hunting her down like a man on a mission.

"Can I have my phone, then?" He held out his hand, looking down at the little device in hers that was being squeezed so tightly that her knuckles were turning white.

Olivia realized her fingers had been clutched tightly around it. She took in a deep breath, released it, and repeated the process until her fingers had relaxed enough for her to let go of the death grip on the phone. Then she passed it on to the man.

"Thank you," she grumbled.

But she wasn't thankful because this man had brought the phone that had disrupted her fairly peaceful day. *How the hell did he even manage that?* Last she checked, she couldn't get any bars as long as she was on the hotel grounds. However, he had one of those old bulky phones with an antenna, so maybe it didn't operate the same as her mobile device.

"Any time!" the man beamed before tipping his hat and leaving as suddenly as he came.

"You look like you are having a bad day," a voice said behind Olivia much later, making her stop.

She had been pacing back and forth around the swimming pool area, trying to shake off the angry energy that had built inside her after speaking with her dad. It was a little hard to do since she usually did this by talking, except she didn't have anyone to talk to. That had angered her even more, and she'd paced some more. If she knew where the gym was, she would have gone there to work off this excess energy.

She turned around to find Nikos standing behind the chair she had sat on a while ago, back when her day was still peaceful. On it was a book she had been pretending to read forever, a wide-brimmed hat that was more to cover her face than to shield her from the sun, and a towel that she'd grabbed from her room.

"I am," she responded. For a brief moment, she had thought about denying it, but what was the point in doing so?

But then she noticed Nikos looked a little haggard himself, for lack of a better word. He had looked so put together and clean when he left this morning, but now, his hair stuck out in different places like he'd run his hands through it repeatedly. His clothes were in disarray, like he'd buttoned and unbuttoned his shirt so many times that the top buttons were barely secured, and his shirt was tucked in weirdly.

"*You* look like you are having a bad day," she threw his words back at him.

"I am." Nikos let out a tired laugh, surprising her that he didn't deny it. *Was he... starting to open up to her?*

"Do you want to talk about it?" she felt compelled to ask as she moved closer to him.

He took a seat where she had been, so she took the next seat, bringing them closer once again. "Do *you* want to talk about it?" Nikos challenged her as he lay down.

"Not really," Olivia smiled as she lay down, too.

"Same." He let out a short laugh that ended with a deep sigh.

The sky was a seamless expanse of clear blue, streaked with white clouds here and there. The sea in front of them stretched out in a beautiful cerulean haze, meeting the sky at a distant point on the horizon. And the sun was just perfect to enjoy a day at the beautiful beach in front of them. Many people were out and about from what she could see as they enjoyed the day in beautiful Santorini. Overall, it was a beautiful day. Or, at least, it should have been a beautiful day, but she couldn't enjoy it.

They sat in comfortable silence for a while, before Nikos suddenly said, "Do you want to go out?"

"Oh?" Olivia asked, her heart suddenly skipping a beat.

"Not like that," Nikos rushed out as he sat back up, compelling Olivia to do the same. "I just meant, like, out of the hotel. I just... I need a distraction, and I think you could use one too."

"Sure," she said without hesitation, ignoring the sinking of her heart that Nikos didn't mean it like *that*.

Did she even want him to mean it like that? That's not something she wanted to dwell on.

It seemed like Nikos was more in a rush to get out of the hotel than she was because, within thirty minutes, they were dressed and out into the vibrant Santorini island—thanks to him asking if she was ready every two minutes.

"What do you want to do?" Nikos asked Olivia as soon as they hit the road and started walking in a random direction.

"I don't know," she said as she looked around, feeling equally elated that they were out of the suffocatingly quiet hotel premises and also very anxious that, at any time, people would see her and start pointing as they had randomly fallen right into a flurry of activity.

All around them were vendors and tourists,

everyone speaking in different languages as they tried to sell and buy from each other. The scent of street food wafted through the air, mixed with the salty smell of the ocean and multiple body odors. *It wasn't as unpleasant as it should be*, Olivia thought.

"Let's take a walk then," he smiled down at her as they continued walking. "Maybe go to a less touristic area."

They'd taken a few steps before Nikos grabbed her around the waist and then maneuvered them so he was standing on the side of the road where vehicles milled about while she walked comfortably on his other side. Olivia looked up at him, taken aback by the gesture, but Nikos just smiled and started pointing out different places to her.

And then, he chose that moment to take her hand in his, so whatever he said was lost on her, since all she could focus on was the warmth that enveloped her at his touch. His hand was warm and comforting. He also held it tight enough for her to feel the strength in his muscles.

Would it be the same in his chest and shoulders? She wondered. She was a sucker for a man who was muscular, but not overpoweringly so. Nikos seemed to fit the bill.

They must have walked for a while, but for all

Olivia knew, they walked only walked a few minutes. By the time she got out of her head long enough to truly take in her surroundings, the night was descending upon them and they were stopping by some benches on a public beach.

"...but then I wouldn't recommend it. As soon as people find out you are not a local, they hike up the prices and you can't tell any difference," Nikos said as he looked down at her, a small smile on his handsome face. Of course, he first helped her sit down before he followed suit, which only increased his charm tenfold in Olivia's mind.

"Yeah," Olivia laughed awkwardly, her face flaming as she was deadly aware of the fact that she did not hear not one thing Nikos had said because her mind was focused on the warm and fuzzy feeling his touch had brought her.

But, then again, she wondered, *what would it be like if he touched more than just* my *hand?*

"Feeling better?" Nikos asked as he sat on the opposite side of her.

"Much better, thanks," she breathed, well aware that she had not thought about her problems once since they decided to leave. And it had to have been gone for a while since the evening sun was almost completely gone from the horizon. "You?"

"Same," Nikos said, giving her the full might of his dimpled smile.

Be still my heart, Olivia thought as she turned away from him, confused by the way her heart skipped a beat at the smallest things this man did. *Is this...? Am I...?*

"I'm hungry though," Nikos said as he looked around like he expected someone at this very busy beach to come rushing to them and offer them food.

Except that is exactly what happened. A man came rushing to them, speaking Greek so rapidly that she could barely understand a word. But he focused entirely on Nikos, leaving Olivia free to look around them.

They were surrounded by a flurry of people, everyone focused on doing their own things, laughing, and some were even dancing to music from a band nearby. There were a lot of vendors here too, so Olivia suspected that they were in a tourist area. Her anxiety about being recognized ratcheted up, her stomach sinking whenever she made eye contact with anyone. Except, the pitchforks and angry mob never actually came, as it looked like everyone was content minding their business.

Maybe it wasn't as bad as her overactive imagination thought.

"And who is this beautiful lady?" she heard the man who had joined them ask, bringing her attention back to the table. He had a very thick accent, which made some of his words hard to hear.

"You!" Olivia hissed as she glared up at the man she now recognized. It was the same person who had come hunting her down with that ugly phone back at the hotel.

"Ahh... Miss Olivia," he smiled down at her like they were long-lost friends. "I am Iossif Lagoulis. Nice to meet you." He went as far as taking his hat off and tipping his head at her. It would have been very charming, except this was the man who thought it okay to bring a stupid phone in a place designed to keep people away from technology.

And, okay, he was conventionally handsome, and dare she say, almost as handsome as Nikos with his warm dark eyes and polite smile, but she refused to acknowledge that.

It's not nice to meet you, she wanted to say, but bit her words back. Nikos was looking at her with a wide smile, like he was delighted the two of them got to meet.

"Nice to meet you too," she let out, albeit with much difficulty. She might have gritted her teeth at some point.

"You are mad at me," he blatantly stated. "That's okay. I'll change that with some free food." And then he was gone as quickly as he had come.

"You've met Iossif?" Nikos asked, not even hiding his smile.

"Unfortunately," Olivia rolled her eyes. *Meeting was a stretch though.*

"Let me guess, he brought a phone so someone could talk to you because they couldn't reach you?"

"How do you know?" she asked, genuinely surprised. *Did they keep tabs on hotel guests like that?*

"That's kind of what he's known for at the Atlantis. Many long-term guests at the hotel are not a big fan of him."

"I can see why." Based on how the Atlantis was designed, people came there to get away from technology, so someone bringing them something that forces them back to technology didn't seem like something people would readily welcome.

"But he's a good man, I promise."

Before she could react, Iossif was back, and in his hands was a large tray. One by one, he put the items in front of them as he proudly announced them.

"Hamburgers, french fries, coleslaw, and some

root beer. Only the best for my American friends," he beamed at them.

Olivia opened her mouth to ask for something a lot less greasy, but Nikos spoke up before she could. "Thank you, Iossif. This looks lovely."

Iossif turned expectantly at Olivia. One look at Nikos told her she should mirror his sentiments. "Yes, this looks lovely," she said with a pained smile.

Iossif looked satisfied with himself. "Now you have to forgive me," he beamed. Thankfully, another group of people captured his attention, and he walked away.

"Seriously?" Olivia muttered as she looked at their food.

"Don't take it personally," Nikos said as he picked up a hamburger. "He means well. His whole thing is about making tourists feel at home, so he runs multiple businesses around that idea. Plus, his food is superb. Here, try it." Nikos handed her the hamburger he had unwrapped.

Olivia took a bite, mainly because she was hungry and this was the only food they had now. Her tongue burst with flavors as spices mixed with something sweet and salty assaulted her senses. She might have let out a tiny moan as she took another bite, completely ignoring Nikos' smug smile.

Olivia was a fine-dining kind of girl. *Only the best for a Clarke.* She couldn't remember the last time she had indulged in junk food and wasn't sure when she'd be able to, so she attacked her food with gusto. They sat in comfortable silence as they devoured their food, down to the last drop of root beer.

"So, tell me about yourself, Miss Olivia Clarke," Nikos said as they both relaxed in their seats.

CHAPTER 8
NIKOS

"**N**o way! That's you?" Nikos asked and then burst out in laughter, his head tipping back and everything.

"I was only a baby!" Olivia tried to glare, but she ended up laughing too.

Nikos was delighted to find out that his favorite commercial of all time, one advertising baby products featuring an adorable giggling baby, was none other than a young Olivia. Meanwhile, it was just embarrassing for her. He said he probably loved the commercial because of the ridiculousness of the ad itself and the stupid but catchy jingle had always made him laugh.

"I can't believe you are the baby from the diaper ad," he said as he calmed down, but then burst into laughter once again at the deadpan look Olivia gave him. "You are iconic around here."

"Iconic is stretching it," she said as she pushed at his shoulder.

He looked beautiful when he laughed. Stop-in-your-steps kind of beautiful.

"No, I'm serious." Nikos grabbed at her and gently squeezed her hand that was still on his shoulder. "You are a legend."

If Olivia didn't know any better, she would think there was awe in his voice. And yet, that is the one thing she had done in her career that everyone seemed to never let her forget. It's why it was the first thing she had mentioned when Nikos asked her the one role she'd been in he'd be surprised by because it was front and center in her mind.

"Well," she swallowed, well aware that Nikos still held her hand on his chest, "my father used to sign me up for anything and everything. I never really had a choice." She'd meant it as a joke, but it came out so pathetic that she wished she could swallow her words.

"If you had the choice, what would you have done?"

That question startled Olivia because no one had ever asked her what she wanted to do. It was almost always expected of her that she would be an actress, and anything other than that was ridiculous.

"I would sing," she said without hesitation. "I've always wanted to be a musician."

"Then, be a musician," he said it like it was that simple.

"It's not that easy," Olivia shook her head and tried to pull her hand back, only for Nikos to hold it tighter. "People would never take me seriously. Everyone thinks everything I have has always been handed to me. If I start singing, I'd be inviting hate on something that I actually love and treasure so much."

"Or, maybe, you'd be inviting love in because you are doing something you enjoy and people get to see the authentic you."

"Not in my world," she whispered, her heart aching. "I was in a musical once and people hated me for it because I got the role over this one actress. She won a singing competition, so everyone had expected she'd get the role of the lead actress. Except, I auditioned and beat her for the role. I was so excited..." She stopped as she remembered how that joy had been snuffed out of her by the paparazzi and angry fans. "That's the last time I ever auditioned for anything or been in a musical. Now, I just get roles because of my family's influence."

Nikos didn't say anything to that. Luckily, Olivia didn't expect him to because, really, what was there to say?

But he finally let her hand go, only to pull her into him in a hug. Her cheek rested on his chest, right where his heart sat, pumping in a gentle and almost soothing rhythm. "No matter how scary it is, Olivia, doing what you want is worth a try."

He didn't say anything more, and she didn't either. Instead, they moved to the sound of the music that had transitioned from the upbeat tempo from before, to now the slow and soothing melody that invited lovers to get lost in each other.

Olivia laid her head on Nikos' chest, letting herself only feel. To feel the warmth that enveloped her when he held her to him. Feel the smoothness of his muscles as her hands went around his waist. Feel the way his heart beat against his chest as he held her close. Feel how his hard length dug into her stomach...

She just wanted to feel.

And it was because of this that she begged, "Please Nikos," once they had returned to the hotel. She wasn't ready to let him go. Not ready to end the night and be left alone with her thoughts once again. She needed him to stay and hold her tonight like she had never needed anyone before.

"If I start, I won't be able to stop," Nikos said as he pulled her to him once again, right outside her bedroom door.

"I don't want you to stop," she whispered as she pulled back to look into his eyes.

He had spent the night touching and caressing her, his lips rubbing her neck, cheeks, and ears, and every touch had her melting. Now... now, she needed *everything*.

Without giving him a chance to react, Olivia grabbed the back of Nikos' head and pulled him to her. He came willingly, their lips meeting in the middle. A rush of adrenaline hit Olivia as intense longing bubbled up in her chest. It had been a while since she'd kissed someone. *Truly kissed them*. Her TV kisses didn't count for shit.

Nikos kissed her like he was a hungry man having his first meal, and at the same time, like he was having his last meal. He savored her, his lips slowly gliding against hers and yet doing it with enough pressure, like he wanted to leave an imprint of himself on her. He held her to him like he was never willing to let her go, and as they moved to her room, he undressed her like a man undressing the most precious present he had ever been given.

Olivia stood in front of Nikos, completely naked and feeling a strong sense of empowerment at the hungry way Nikos' eyes traced her naked body. They didn't need the lights. The moon overhead provided enough light through the open balcony and windows.

"Olivia," he rasped as he adjusted his very hard length.

It stood at attention, calling to her, so she moved closer to him. Olivia made sure he had an eye full of her curves, exaggerating the sway of her hips until she stood right in front of him. "Call me, Liv," she whispered, tracing her fingers over his chest.

She had been right. He was muscular, but not in the overpowering sense. She savored the rush that came over her when he shuddered under the ministrations of her fingers as she took off his shirt one button at a time. He held her gaze, and she was giddy to know that his pupils were completely dilated.

"Fuck," Nikos hissed when her fingers made contact with the zipper of his pants.

The front was slightly soaked from his leaking length. The anticipation of having him inside of her made her release a moan as she rubbed her legs together. She was wetter than she could ever remember being. Her clit pulsed at the thought of getting contact with the warm, hard length she now held in her hands, and her center clenched when she thought how good he would feel sliding inside her.

Olivia let out a deeper moan this time, her eyes rolling into the back of her head just from the picture her mind had conjured up. Her entire body was alight with need and hot as anticipation built in her stomach.

She had initially intended on teasing him with her lips and hands, but that all went out of the window as her body begged her to take the pleasure it craved.

"Nikos, I need you," she moaned as her legs shook, giving way from under her.

Nikos held her up, whispering, "I got you." And then he gave her a kiss that was almost punishing. With a strength that was extremely arousing, he lifted her so her legs wrapped around him.

They both let out simultaneous moans when her wet center slid right onto his leaking shaft. Nikos pulled Olivia's hair out of her face, held it in a fist behind her back, and then started moving her slowly on his length. Her lower lips wrapped around him, making both shudder as his member rubbed at her pulsing clit.

Olivia pulled back from the kiss with a gasp and then started moving herself. "I need you," she moaned as she looked him right in the eyes. She hoped he could see how much she needed this—*needed him*—and that he would give her everything she needed.

"I don't have condoms," Nikos said, holding her so she would stop moving.

"Don't need it. I'm clean." She didn't stop moving. Couldn't stop moving because Nikos felt so good rubbing against her clit. "Are you?"

She *needed* him inside her.

"I am," he said as he held her waist much tighter, pulling her to him so there wasn't much room for her to move. "Are you sure, Liv?"

"Please," she gasped, especially shaking at the way he growled her name.

As if that was all the invitation he needed, he moved them to the bed with a swiftness she didn't see coming, then buried himself in her right to the hilt. Olivia let out a short, ecstatic scream as she arched her back off the bed. Her insides shuddered at how full she felt, and she almost couldn't believe that he had finally entered her. He felt full and warm, and just so big sheathed in her warmth.

"Fuck, you're so tight," Nikos hissed as he pulled back and cradled her face. "Are you okay?"

"Don't stop," she whispered as she wrapped her legs around him and pulled him back until he was inside her all the way once again.

Nikos grabbed her hair once again and didn't move until she was looking right at him. As soon as she did, she couldn't look away, as he looked like he was silently begging her to look at him.

There was a heightened sense of intimacy in an already intimate act when that happened. Olivia could see every emotion that rushed over him as he moved inside her reflected in his eyes and the tightness of his jaw. She could see the wonder, the lust, the joy, and maybe it was wishful thinking on her end, but she could see a little love and awe.

It was when he increased his tempo just a little bit that Olivia knew she was a goner. He was selfless in how he pleasured her, even more so with how he worshiped her body as his fingers caressed her body with the same care his length caressed her inner walls. Olivia gave it back as good as she got it, wanting him to feel the same reverence he was worshiping her body with. She touched him with her fingers and mirrored his movements, wanting to communicate how good he made her body feel without words.

He made her cum first before he even thought about letting himself enjoy what they were doing together. His stamina was quite admirable because he kept up the same speed until he was well and truly ready to cum. His hand shifted between them, searching for her engorged pleasure button. As soon as he found it, he rubbed her with precise movements that mirrored the increase in his movements.

Olivia couldn't handle the overload of feeling anymore, so she threw her head back and came once again. As if that was the permission Nikos had needed, he followed her right over the edge—and, through it all, they maintained eye contact.

Olivia held onto this moment like it was all that had ever existed and will ever exist as she forgot everyone and everything.

FIVE HOURS.

It took Olivia all of five hours since she woke up for her newfound peace to be disturbed.

"No, Dad, I did not," she said through clenched teeth.

"Then, how come I got a call that the role is going to be given to someone else?" her father accused her.

"Gee, I don't know. Maybe because your *daughter* is involved in a scandal right now?" Olivia put emphasis on the word 'daughter' as a reminder to her father of who she was to him.

"That's nonsense and it will blow over soon," he brushed her off.

"When?" she asked. "W*hen* will this blow over, Dad? Hmm? Because you said the same thing when it first happened weeks ago. That I'm still here means it hasn't *blown over*."

"It will blow over," he insisted. "People will find something else to talk about. They always do."

"Maybe if you just let me address this? Clear the air..." she said hopefully.

"Absolutely not!" Her father growled down the line. "You will do no such thing. Do you hear me?"

Olivia bit back every harsh word she wanted to say, fighting herself from telling her father to shove it and that he didn't run her life. Except, he *did* run her life.

"Do I make myself clear?" he shouted when she didn't respond.

"Yes, sir," Olivia responded with great difficulty as a ringing rose in her head.

Her father might have said some more things, but she wasn't sure because she couldn't hear anything beyond the pounding of her head. Her eyes stung with tears, her throat growing scratchy as she held back from breaking down.

This is what she always felt like whenever she spoke to her father. Like she was a little girl who didn't know the first thing about running her own life, even if she was twenty-three now. She hated it so much because she knew what it was like to be close to her dad. They'd had a beautiful relationship, but that felt like lifetimes ago.

"Can I have my phone back?" Iossif said, his deep voice breaking through the ringing in her head.

Olivia pulled it from her ear, only to find that her father had long hung up. Without saying anything, she handed the phone back to Iossif, then turned around, and left him standing in the kitchen where he had found her. He said words, but she was not in the mood to talk to anyone.

Maybe if Nikos was around, but he had long left to handle his own affairs.

Olivia was, once again, reminded that the one person who had always been her sounding board, the only person who could understand the pressure her father put on her, was not accessible to her at the moment.

That bad reminder did nothing but make her want to release the tears she struggled to keep at bay as she climbed the stairs, unwilling to cry. She had much experience with this, and yet, the burn in her throat was something she never got used to.

She ended up wandering into the entertainment room she hadn't made much use of, although she had already been in there to know what she needed. In the corner sat a grand piano that looked rarely used, even if the room was just as clean as all the rooms in the house were. Without thinking much of it, she moved toward the piano, her fingers itching to bring her the comfort and expression only music ever had.

As soon as her hands started strumming the keys, a lightness settled over her like her body knew it was about to have the release she craved. Soon, words accompanied the haunting melody she played as she finally let her feelings out.

CHAPTER 9
NIKOS

Nikos' day had been as stressful as it had been long. He woke up intent on writing his final report on the hotel, running numbers, checking the finances, and inspecting the hotel from top to bottom. However, his inspection had made him less and less enthusiastic about the idea of selling.

But he had to sell, right? Yeah, he had to. Everything was already on track, and there was no reason to stop now.

Still, that did not improve his mood one bit, making a long day even longer as the good mood he'd woken up with waned until he couldn't remember why he'd even woken up happy and feeling lighter than he had in days. So, by the time he made it back into his house late in the evening, he was beat and just about ready to turn in, even if the sun had only just gone over the horizon.

A melancholy melody seemed to echo within the very walls of his house greeted him. If he didn't know any better, he would think his house was haunted, but his night out with Olivia yesterday had clued him into the fact that she loved to sing.

To be honest, when she told him she loved to sing, Nikos had pictured music we get lost in every once in a while in the privacy of our bathrooms as we had an impromptu one-person concert.

But, no, this was not that. It was way beyond that.

This music transported you to places you've been before, places you've never been, and those you've never even thought about being. Suddenly, the weariness in his bones seemed to slip away as he followed the sound of her singing, like a siren beckoning a sailor into the darkest depths of the ocean.

He found Olivia in the entertainment room he had pointedly ignored for most of his life. The memories of him and his parents in the room never let him stay in there for long. And yet, he couldn't stop his feet from dragging him into the cozy room, mesmerized by the picture before him.

Olivia sat at the grand piano, singing a song he didn't know as her hands strummed the keys with expert precision. She looked quite spectacular as she was in a shirt he recognized as his, her hair pulled into a bun on top of her head, giving him the perfect view of her silhouette.

Yet, his attention was more drawn to her words. Her song was sorrowful, full of regret and pain. He felt a powerful urge to go hug her and protect her from everything that had ever hurt her. She had her head tilted back like she hoped the heavens could hear her pain. It was when he saw the tears slip out that he could no longer stand the fact that she was in pain. So Nikos moved with purpose toward her.

Maybe he made a noise, he wasn't sure, but Olivia let out a gasp as she stopped singing and playing the piano, her head whipping back in time to see him bend down and engulf her in his arms. She let out a second gasp, and he expected her to pull away, except that she put her arms around him and let out a sob.

Nikos held her tightly, hoping to comfort her as she let out all the pain he had heard. He shifted, so he sat on the bench she had vacated, pulling her to straddle him. Her hair was falling out of the bun, so he released it and ran his fingers through it instead, stroking her hair in the same gentle manner he rubbed her back.

It might have been a minute or an hour later when she finally stopped, but it could have also been longer since the sun was now gone and the moon made her appearance.

"Sorry," Olivia crooned as she leaned back from him, rubbing her face. "I don't know what came over me."

"Hey," he called when she refused to make eye contact with him. "It's okay."

"You don't have to say that," she whispered as she tried to get off him, but Nikos held her tighter until she stopped moving.

"Olivia," he called, but she refused to look at him. "Liv," he tried again, gently, as he tilted her face until she was looking at him, "it's okay." He emphasized every word to ensure she understood he didn't fault her for crying. His fingers moved back to rub her hair and back as he tried to give her as much comfort as possible.

Her face was blotched and red, and maybe she thought it was off-putting because she tried to hide away again, but he wouldn't let her. She had never looked more beautiful.

Earlier in the day, he might have caved and

made a quick Google search about her. She definitely looked more put together in the pictures he saw than he had ever seen her in person. She looked almost too perfect and untouchable. But here, with him now, Olivia seemed to have let her guard down and show her authentic self without the makeup that hid her freckles and, somehow, always red face, fake smiles that didn't reach her beautiful green eyes, and forced emotions. It was a beautiful thing.

His search had taken him to two articles that had given him a general idea of why she might have been hiding at his hotel. He could only imagine how it felt having people say what they were saying about her.

"Thank you," Olivia said eventually as another tear fell down her already tear-blotched face.

He cupped her face again and rubbed the errant tear away, then leaned in and kissed where he had just rubbed. When he felt Olivia practically melting into him, he turned her face so he could kiss the other side, and then he kissed her cheek and the other. She let out a soft giggle when he kissed her forehead, so he leaned down and kissed her cute button nose, at which point she truly laughed.

Maybe it was the effects of the singing, but her laughter sounded so musical that Nikos wanted to hear it again. So he leaned over and repeated his movements until she was squirming with laughter.

His long and exhausting day had melted away, and in its place was the pleasantness of this moment. He'd never been one to spend "quality time" with women like this—with people, really. Always on the move, wanting to move from one task to the next, and yet Olivia made him want to stop and take in the moment. He wanted to enjoy it with her.

She looked radiant now, where she had looked broken and exhausted before. He had never noticed, but when she truly smiled, she squinted her nose, and at the top of her lips were two tiny holes that added to the beauty of her smile. Being this close to her, he also noticed the tiny dusting of freckles on her face, which weren't as visible from a distance and turned darker when she blushed as hard as she was right now.

"Do you want to play again?" Nikos asked as he gestured to the piano, hoping that she would say yes. He *really* wanted to hear her sing once again.

"I've never really played for anyone before," she said as she looked away, her ears reddening.

"Tell you what," he said as he shifted them so she had her back to his front. "If you sing, I'll play."

He turned them around, so they were both facing the piano.

This angle was a tight fit, and yet Nikos was determined to make it work, not wanting to leave this moment just yet. She smelled like apples and cinnamon, a very heady combination. He had an incredible urge to keep her in his arms as long as possible, and he wasn't going to fight it. *Didn't want to fight it.*

Before Olivia could protest, he started to play the only song he knew how to play on the piano—*Jingle Bells*. Olivia let out a delightful giggle that settled right into his erratic heart. He closed his eyes to soak in the sound as he continued to play, unaware of the big smile that split his lips.

Thankfully, she humored him by singing the whole song, and maybe, just maybe, *Jingle Bells* was now Nikos' favorite song. The ridiculousness of the song had brought a lightheartedness to the moment, making Nikos grateful to his *Yiayia* for insisting he learn how to play the song way back when they'd needed someone to play the piano for a Christmas thing.

Oliva turned back to him like she wanted to say something to him, but Nikos was suddenly overcome with the need to kiss her. He leaned in, cradled her head, and kissed her in a manner that was meant to bruise and leave the memory of him with her for a while.

She pulled back after a few hot seconds, gasping for breath, eyes frantically searching his. "What was that for?" she asked as she touched her red lips with her fingers.

"You are very beautiful, Liv," he whispered, feeling the need to let her know what he felt.

Her widened eyes made him feel like, maybe, he shouldn't have said that, and yet it was the truth. She *was* beautiful.

"Thank you," she whispered, but looked away from him.

"What's wrong?" he asked as he noticed the tension that had suddenly built up in her shoulders.

"Nothing," she rushed out, but he could feel her pull away mentally, as if his comment had unsettled her.

"Talk to me, baby." He maneuvered them until she was now straddling him. With one hand gently supporting her, he caressed her face and waited for her to make eye contact. "What's the problem? Did I say something wrong?"

"It's not you," she eventually sighed, her gaze dropping for a moment before meeting his again.

"It's just... everyone who has ever called me 'beautiful' has always ended it, with 'just like your mother'."

An array of emotions ran across her eyes too fast for Nikos to identify all of them. But more central to all was disdain, longing, and deep sadness. It drained all the color she had a few minutes ago when she was happy, and he hated that look on her.

"You're more than just a reflection of your mother," Nikos said, knowing that he had never once thought of her as anything but Olivia Clarke, a woman who he thought was a nuisance just a few days ago but also turned out to be his greatest source of comfort.

"You probably don't know much about my mother then," she shrugged off his comment as she looked away.

"Hey, I mean it," he made sure she was looking at him, "you might look like her, but that doesn't mean you are not your own person. You're not bound by her shadow."

Nikos wished he could say more about her, but he knew he didn't know her enough to say anything more than what he had seen. And yet, based on what he knew, there was no way a woman like Olivia faded into anyone's shadow.

She was brilliant. Everything about her capti-vated him, and he had noticed the same thing yesterday when they were out. She had an aura about her that drew you in when she was truly happy and free. He had only seen glimpses of the real her here and there, and she was truly electric. Just that was enough to let him know she was a woman of her own caliber. No matter how much the world was beating her up, she shined when she let herself.

"But, I am." She shook her head. "Everywhere I go, it's always about my mother and whether or not I can live up to her legacy. I just want to be seen for who I am, not just as an extension of her."

"Then, show them, baby," he said. "Show them you are not just your mother's daughter."

"It's not that easy," she claimed, shaking her head.

"Why not?"

She kept quiet for a while, biting her lip and looking deep in thought. Nikos waited patiently. "I don't think people want to see me for me. I've... I've done things. Bad things," she whispered.

"So bad that you can't fix them?" he asked gently, rubbing her hair from her face when she tried to hide behind it.

"So bad that I had to hide out here," she sighed, a mixture of regret and frustration in her voice as she grabbed and pulled at her hair instead of hiding behind it.

"What happened?" He gently pulled her hands away and held them on their sides so she wasn't pulling her hair.

She hesitated, looking at him hopefully with a hint of fear. Before he could tell her she didn't have to tell him, she started talking.

"I was so stupid," she stated. "I was hanging out with this group. The bad kind, I guess you could say. My best friend, Ava, had warned me about them, but they had said some things that made me want to prove them wrong."

"What did they say?" he asked, trying to encourage her to keep talking. He rubbed her hands with smooth circles, noticing that this made her stiff shoulders relax just a little bit.

"They called me a goody-two-shoes—like my mother," Olivia confessed, letting out a bitter laugh that was so unlike her. "They said I was too sheltered, and I didn't have a worry in the world because everything I had has always been handed to me." Nikos listened intently, allowing her to tell her story without interruptions. "I was stupid—so stupid. Ava tried to tell me that they just wanted a reaction out of me, but I didn't listen. I was mad, Nikos, so freaking mad. No one sees me," her voice broke. "They all think I'm just this spoiled person who had it easy and was too stuck up. And I wanted to show them that I wasn't. So, I did and said some things I shouldn't have."

Nikos waited patiently as she gathered herself. He watched her trying to fight her breakdown, wanting to give her more comfort than what he did, but he knew she had to work through this on her own.

"I didn't know that they were recording me. They dared me to do all kinds of things and I did without hesitation—until I realized that they had been live streaming the entire night. I panicked and said some more things, because I thought it would divert their attention, but it did the opposite. Ava tried to get me to stop, but I couldn't. I was panicking and then I turned my attention to her."

"She's the daughter of a major producer, you see. But his movies have been struggling and their family is broke, but they had been parading around like nothing was wrong. Her father is all about his image and he just kept sinking his family into heavy debt because he wants everyone to think he's still this rich person. I let it all out." She hung her head in shame as the gravity of what she had done sank in for Nikos.

"You exposed your best friend?"

"That's not even the worst part," she whispered, as if she was afraid of the words she was saying. This time, he let her hang her head, as she clearly needed a minute.

"What's worse than that?" Nikos held his breath.

"Our family publicist released a statement saying that Ava had drugged me and was the reason for my 'erratic behavior'."

"Oh, Liv."

"I tried to fix it," she cried. "I really did. But, my father won't let me. He had people monitor everything I did for a while before he shipped me off here. And now, he acts like nothing's happening. Ava took all the brunt of this scandal when she shouldn't have." The vulnerability in her voice exposed the wounds that still festered beneath the surface. "I'm a coward, Nikos. I'm such a coward. I ran away when I should have stayed and faced the backlash alongside my best friend."

"You are not a coward," he said. "You made a mistake. A terrible mistake that, maybe, you couldn't handle or fix at the moment. But you will, won't you?"

"I want to." She grabbed at his shirt desperately, like she needed him to believe she wasn't the person she appeared to be. "I want to fix it, but my father—"

"Screw your father," he interrupted her. "What do *you* want, Liv? Do you want this to be held against you for the rest of your life?"

"No, I want this to be fixed. I want my best friend back." The death grip on his shirt lessened, but she didn't let go.

"Then you'll figure it out. I know you will. You need to believe in yourself, not in the expectations or judgment of others. It won't be easy. Trust me, I know. But you'll find a way to make amends."

For some reason, Nikos felt the need to tell her he understood a thing or two about familiar obligations and how suffocating they can be. He told her about his own issues, like how he had been burdened with expectations of running the hotel and how hard he had tried to run away from that by making an entirely new life for himself in America. It felt good to let it all out and tell someone who could understand how much expectations weighed on someone, especially when it didn't feel like you were given a choice in the matter.

"I can't decide if selling is the best option," he said, surprising himself with this declaration. He was pretty solid about selling a few days ago, but now he wasn't so sure. The heaviness that had been weighing on him since his last conversation with *Papous* was still there, and it was enough to have him try to reconsider this decision.

Even if he tried not to, Nikos had been hit by memories of his good time at the hotel, and revisiting everything with Olivia right now helped give him a clarity he hadn't had in a while. He now knew he was making a rushed decision because he had always craved something more than the hotel, and yet, this craving had blinded him from making the right choices when it came to The Atlantis.

"You need to make a decision too, baby," he said gently. "At some point, you'll have to face the consequences. Do you want your reputation to be someone who runs and brushes things under the rug?" Knowing a bit about Olivia's family and their tendency to avoid public confrontations, Nikos posed a pointed question. "Is that the person you want to be?"

She hesitated once again, but admitted, "No. I

want to be better. This whole thing has been eating me up for weeks since I can't talk to anyone about it. I just want it to stop."

Nikos offered a piece of advice born from his slowly blooming clarity. "Maybe this is where you need to pave your own path, even if it's from your family. It's not easy, but it might be what you need to do for yourself."

And maybe Nikos had to take his own advice and actually tell *Papous* that he was not ready to take on the burden of managing the hotel. Maybe they could talk and come up with a solution that works for both of them because the decision to sell had been born out of a need to find liberation from managing The Atlantis. However, he wasn't sure that was something *Papous* would welcome, as it definitely was not the right move for the hotel.

"I see you for you, Liv," he told her, cupping her face. "Beautiful, not because of anyone else. Beautiful because of who you are. You need to believe that you can be your own woman outside your family name and legacy." He leaned in and kissed her on her forehead.

CHAPTER 10
OLIVIA

O livia felt light and just a little happier. More than she had been in weeks, anyway. The gloomy heaviness that had been dragging her down since her mistake made headlines had cleared some, and so the wheels in her head were spinning.

Could she really make this work? Would she dare go against her father's wishes?

Nikos' lips on her forehead added to the feeling of lightness she was experiencing. He had surprised her since he came into the room when she was singing. She didn't know what to expect from him, as every move he had made was so unlike the man she had thought he was. Yet, she had loved every second. She couldn't remember ever wanting to be this close to someone of the opposite sex. But with Nikos, she never wanted to leave this little cocoon he had created for them.

It was safe. And she needed safety.

It was dark outside and the only light they had was from the automatic lights outside the house, which switched on as soon as it got dark. This was all Olivia had to see Nikos' face. The darkness from the inside battled with the small light from the outside, giving him a mysterious and almost comical look.

She would have liked to stay in the moment for much longer, except her rumbling stomach reminded her she had not eaten in a hot minute.

Nikos pulled back in surprise, and they both burst out in laughter as they came back to earth. "Let's go grab something to eat," he said as he finally dislodged them.

Olivia's legs wobbled for a second for a lack of use, but Nikos supported her as he led her outside the room.

"I can't imagine why you'd want to sell off this beautiful place," Olivia randomly commented as she remembered what Nikos had said before. They were moving toward the dining area and the sound of the other guests made her stomach roll. But she didn't want to run away like she had been since she came. So, she held her head high, ignoring the hushed whispers and pointing from the people she passed.

Brush it off, Olivia, brush it off.

"Well, the financial burden is too much," he said in a way that made Olivia think he had rehearsed this one too many times.

"Financial burden?" She arched an eyebrow up at him, completely ignoring his arm around her or the fact that his fingers were rubbing her back in the same manner he had been earlier.

He hesitated, turning to glance down at her before he said, "Well, the upkeep of the hotel, maintenance costs, and other expenses—it's a lot to handle."

"Then think about cost-effective solutions," Olivia said, her mind racing. "Maybe you can look at more service offerings to attract more guests, cut down unnecessary costs..." she trailed off when he turned at her with a raised eyebrow.

"It's a combination of things, Liv." He rubbed a hand down his face and, for the first time since she met him, she realized how weary he looked.

Olivia badly wanted to make him feel better like he had made her, so she tried to think of solutions for him. "Things like what?" she asked him, totally trying to ignore the butterflies in her stomach from the way Nikos was calling her Liv.

But he didn't respond—at least, not right away.

They moved to get their food, Olivia painfully aware of the criticism being sent her way in the buzzing dining area, yet she ignored it all as she tried to keep her focus on Nikos and the food they were getting. Thankfully, Nikos led them outside to the side of the hotel grounds she hadn't ventured to yet.

It was a quaint garden with gazebos all around that were designed for privacy. They took one furthest from everyone, and only then did Nikos speak. "I'm afraid of the burnout," he said, his focus on his plate of food. "I once witnessed it with my father and granddad, and it was not pretty..." He lingered like he had more to say, but shook his head and stopped for a moment.

Olivia tried to think of what to say, but before she could, Nikos continued.

"More than anything," he sighed, "there's this feeling that the place doesn't have the same charm it used to. I'm afraid that I'll hate being back here full-time."

"I think it's not really about the place changing, but maybe how you are viewing it," she stated, well aware that she had felt the same about her child-hood home right before it was turned into the cold museum it is now.

"Maybe," Nikos said, though he didn't sound convinced.

"Alright, how about this?" Olivia tried. "How about I show you what I see? You know, just so you have a different perspective of the hotel? Maybe that will help."

Nikos looked at her for a minute, his head tilted like he was trying to figure her out.

"Why do you care enough to help me gain a different perspective?" He looked genuinely confused, like he couldn't understand why she would do that.

"Well, you helped me out, and now I think it's time to help you, too. You said The Atlantis doesn't hold the same charm, but all I see is charm. Let me help you."

Nikos didn't look completely on board with Olivia's idea, but he went with it, letting her drag him every which way around the hotel as she told him about what she thought about the building.

She started by pointing out what she liked about the hotel and, at Nikos' insistence, she also told him what she thought could change. He took it all in stride with a thoughtful look on his face that didn't clear until long after their tour, but she had no way of knowing if it was a good thing or a bad thing.

"Do you really want to let all this go?"

Those had been Olivia's words to Nikos after their impromptu tour around the hotel last night.

It was quite interesting to see the hotel through fresh eyes. Last night had cemented him into the idea that selling was *definitely* not the way to go and she'd actually come up with some ideas about what he should do.

He had also fully embraced and welcomed the memories of his parents that he had tried to ignore for so long, which made him realize that this was also part of the reason he wanted to sell. He couldn't go a corner without recognizing something from his childhood, which made it really hard for him to enjoy being at The Atlantis.

Nikos had been using any excuse he could find to avoid facing his old life here, along with the things he lost when he lost his mother and father. However, their memories were still alive. He suddenly wasn't so scared to face any of that. And once he welcomed the fact that his parents' memories would always remain alive in the hotel, he realized he hadn't been seeing it in its grandiose splendor.

For the first time since he got here, he was now one hundred percent ready to talk with *Papous* about the next steps. He'd spent the past few hours in the *Papous*' office since he wasn't using it as often since Nikos arrived.

Nikos worked on his ideas, putting everything down so he could have a conversation with *Papous* after running the numbers. Right as he was done with his presentation, there was a knock at the door.

Papous opened the door before he responded and, right as he went to say something, a man he recognized walked in. His heart sank as he was met first with the gleeful look of the buyer he had been in touch with, then *Papous*' disappointed glare.

"Mr. Kappellis," the man said in glee as he moved toward Nikos, completely ignoring the older Kappellis next to him. "I was very glad for the images and proposal you sent. I had to come and see the place for myself." Not once did Nikos look away from *Papous*. "I wanted to discuss the details of the sale in person." He stood in front of Nikos now, forcing him to gaze down at the old and short, pudgy man.

"Mr. Antov," Nikos said, forcing a smile. "I wasn't expecting you so soon." He stole a glance at *Papous*, whose disappointment had not wavered one bit.

"After those images you sent, I had to come. As you know, I am very keen on closing this acquisition as soon as possible. Shall we run the numbers?"

"Yes, about that," Nikos started, stopping Mr. Antov from taking a seat. "I'm afraid the deal is off."

Nikos missed the surprised look from Mr. Antov, looking back at *Papous* hoping he would understand.

"Excuse me?" The shout from Mr. Antov brought his attention back to the man. "What do you mean the deal's off? Is it a money thing? Do you need more? Because I'm willing to double the original price."

"It's not a money thing," he responded in barely sealed irritation. He did not have time for this!

"We had an agreement, Kappellis," the man finally lost it. "You sent me the pictures just yesterday!" Spittle came from the side of his mouth as he glared at Nikos, but that was nothing. *His glare was nothing.*

Nikos looked back to *Papous* to find him shaking

his head, a deep frown marring his tired face before he turned and walked out of the office after one last look at Mr. Antov. His heart sank, hating the look he saw on his grandfather.

The last time *Papous* gave Nikos *that* look was when he left Greece, even after a long time of fighting and back and forth with his grandparents. For the longest time, he and Papous had not seen eye to eye, but they had fixed their relationship. That they might be back in the same place bothered Nikos so much.

He moved to follow him, only to remember the other man in the room.

"I understand the inconvenience this has caused, Mr. Antov, and I apologize you came all this way for no reason. However, after careful consideration, I've come to the conclusion that I will not be selling. I hope you understand." He hoped his corporate voice would help him gain control of this situation, but he didn't stay around long enough to find out. He rushed out of the room, ignoring Mr. Antov's perplexed look.

"Understand?" he heard the man respond as he tried to follow him outside. "I should sue you..." The rest of the words faded away because Nikos was rushing down the hall faster than Mr. Antov could keep up, heading to his grandparent's house where he hoped he'd find *Papous*.

He found him sitting in the living room, a deep frown etched on his face as he looked off into the distance.

"*Papous*, I—I wanted to sell," he admitted, even if he wanted to lie his way out of this. "I thought selling the hotel would be the best option for us, but... I've had time to think and I know now that it's not the best option."

"What's best for us, or what's best for *you*?" *Papous* challenged, still not turning around to look at him.

"Best for me," Nikos hung his head as all the adrenaline that had fueled him in the past few minutes drained out of his body. "I'm sorry," he added uselessly.

Papous didn't respond or turn around to look at him.

CHAPTER II
NIKOS

It took at least five days for Nikos to get another opportunity to speak with *Papous*. Not for a lack of trying either.

The man had intentionally changed the subject when Nikos had tried to branch the subject or he just wasn't able to get him alone. Even now, as they had lunch together, Nikos was unable to get *Papous* to look at him, no matter how many times he made conversation that was, more often than not, pointed toward the older gentleman.

It had taken him a while to get rid of Mr. Antov. It had taken him even longer to convince the man not to sue, although Nikos wasn't sure he had any grounds to stand on for wanting to sue. Even then, it was better to not have to deal with that if he didn't have to.

"So, about the hotel—" he started as soon as he saw an opening when *Yiayia* cleared the plates.

"Not now," *Papous* glared at him in a hushed whisper, his eyes following *Yiayia's* movements in the kitchenette.

However, Nikos had had enough with *Papous* not wanting to talk to him, so he pushed. "We need to talk about this! I wasn't going to sell—"

"Walk with me," *Papous* pinned him with a glare, then abruptly stood up, heading to *Yiayia*.

He whispered something to her that made her smile, and then she turned around to give him a hug. Nikos looked away from their intimate moment, as always, feeling like a little boy eavesdropping on something he shouldn't be.

Papous didn't wait for him. He turned, picked up *Yiayia's* flower vase that sat in the middle of the kitchen island, and walked out the door. Nikos was off his feet and out the door too, not wanting to lose *Papous* again.

They walked to the side of the house with the flowerbed *Papous* had built for *Yiayia* all those years ago. Bending down, the older man picked up some flowers, replaced them in the water vase, and then went back inside without a word.

A few minutes later, he came back outside, and he made his way toward the beach. Nikos' stomach twisted in uncomfortable knots as he realized they were finally going to talk. When Nikos was younger, he would quietly follow his dad and *Papous* around as they worked around the hotel. This felt extremely like that, except now he was following *Papous,* not because he was observing him at work but because he had done something extremely offensive in *Papous'* eyes.

"I wanted to sell," Nikos said, unable to take the silence. "When I came back here, I did want to sell because I didn't want to run the hotel. But, that's changed, *Papouli*." He thought about giving his reasons why he didn't want to run the hotel, but every one of them sounded a lot like an excuse. "I have ideas," he added when *Papous* didn't acknowledge him, "ideas that I wanted to run by you."

And yet again, *Papous* didn't respond. It was five more minutes of walking and Nikos was about to ask if *Papous* had heard him before he halted.

"Turn around," *Papous* instructed, his eyes not reaching Nikos. He obediently turned around, wondering what was going on inside *Papous'* mind.

"When I was a little boy," *Papous* started, "my father told me about how I would, one day, run this hotel. It's something that I've always known. Something that I always took pride in."

"What—"

"You see, Nikos," *Papous* didn't let him interrupt. "This hotel," he paused as he gestured to the grand structure they were facing, "it wasn't always in the Kappellis name. There was a time when my grandfather, your great-great-grandfather, lost the hotel. He was tricked out of ownership and he spent years fighting to get it back. It changed ownership in the course of eighteen years and, each time, they changed how it looked. Each time, they chipped away at what this hotel was supposed to be, a sanctuary for people looking to get away from the craziness of their lives. So, when my grandfather got the hotel back, he asked my father to promise that it would remain in the Kappellis name. My father made me promise too, swearing that the hotel would remain in our family name."

"To you, these might look like just buildings to auction off," *Papous* made a sweep of the hotel that they were now facing. "But, to me, it's our entire family history. I was only a boy when my father renovated the hotel to what you see now. It used to be mortar and brick, but he wanted more. So, he changed the hotel to what it is today."

Nikos had listened intently, wondering what point his *Papous* was trying to make and when he'd give him a chance to convince him, once again, that he changed his mind about selling.

"This hotel is the Kappellis legacy," a small smile played on *Papous*' lips, but it disappeared as fast as it had come. "This is our home," and then he was frowning, "our history." He stopped talking, eyes sweeping across the grand structures of The Atlantis like he was taking it in for the first time.

As if in slow motion, Nikos watched *Papous* trying but failing to not break down. He swallowed multiple times, his Adam's apple bobbing up and down with the motion as his eyes blinked rapidly. *Papous*' hands shook before he curled them into a fist, then turned around at Nikos.

"You want to sell the hotel? I'm not stopping you," his voice broke and so did Nikos' heart. "That is *your* choice as the new owner. But I made a promise to my father that it would stay in our family for as long as I lived. So, here is what I'd like *you* to promise *me*," he pinned Nikos with an unwavering stare even as moisture gathered in his eyes. "Promise that you will wait until your *Yiayia* and I are six feet under, *then* you can sell. Allow me the chance to die, knowing that I fulfilled a promise I made to my father all those years ago. Please, don't make a liar out of me."

Before Nikos could gather his wits about him, *Papous* turned around and headed back to where they came from.

Nikos watched him go, unable to process what just happened and the fact that he'd just witnessed his papous breakdown for the first time in years. The last time he had shown that much emotion, he'd lost his son.

"WHAT?" came a snippy voice from the other end of the line.

"Oh, hi, Ava," Olivia said, surprised that Ava had finally picked up.

She had spent the past few days trying to get in touch with her former best friend. The first time she had called, Ava had picked up, but once she realized it was her, she had hung up quickly. Olivia was borrowing Iossif's phone since she tried speaking with Ava.

Ava didn't respond, but she didn't hang up either.

So, progress?

"How have you been?" Olivia asked, tapping her fingers nervously on the bench she had sat on with Nikos the day they went out.

"Seriously?" Ava scoffed. "What do you want, Clarke?"

There was a hint of hostility in Ava's voice, but Olivia could hear the note of sadness and exhaustion in her voice, which was enough to tell her how Ava was.

"I wanted to apologize," she started. Ava didn't respond. "I'm so sorry, Ava. About everything."

"Is that all?" Ava asked when Olivia stalled. She wasn't sure where to even start.

"I—I..."

"Well, if that is all then, have a good day, Clarke."

"Wait! Wait! Please," Olivia pleaded in desperation, not wanting to lose her friend again.

"This apology is a little too late," Ava interrupted whatever Olivia had to say. "If you were sorry, you would have been here with me, helping me fix this mess you created. But you left!"

"No, I—"

"You left me." Those three words were laced with a lot of pain and betrayal that hit Olivia right in her heart. "You left me to face the world alone."

"Ava, I had no choice," Olivia tried.

"Yes, you did. You could have taken me with you. You could have told me where you were going and asked me to come—but you didn't." Olivia was full-on crying now, as was Ava on the other side of the line. People around looked at her like she was crazy, but she didn't care. Not when her best friend was breaking down on the other end of the line and she wasn't there to hug her.

"You're not a cruel person, Olivia. I know you're not. The things you exposed about my father that night, I wanted to tell the world, too. Don't get me wrong, the way you went about it was all wrong and it shouldn't have come out the way it did, but I was ready for the world to know because I was tired of the façade Papa forces onto the family. But then, your family accused me of drugging you and you didn't say anything? You just ran away?"

"Ava..." that was all Olivia was able to get out between hiccups.

"We promised to face everything together, remember?" Ava's voice broke. "Back in high school with Timothy Clayton? I was with you throughout that entire scandal. We escaped together to my family's ranch, and we made that promise. Do you remember what you said to me?" she asked, sniffing on the other end as she shuffled around.

"You said, '*No matter what happens, we'll always be there for each other. We're a team, Ava, through thick and thin*'," Ava quoted Olivia's words to her, which were shared between two scared kids who had no one but each other to rely on for comfort.

"I meant every word," she pleaded, "I just... I don't know..."

"I could have forgiven you for a lot of things, but not that. You left me. Why did you leave?"

"I had to," Olivia said, uselessly.

"I'd had the longest day with people harassing my family, so I visited my best friend. Only, I was told that you left. They wouldn't even tell me where you went. Just that you were gone and I should stay away from you."

Olivia's voice cracked as she replied, "I know I can't undo what's done, but I want to make things right. I want to be there for you now, Ava. I miss you, and I'm so sorry for leaving you behind. I'm sorry for not calling you sooner."

"What can you do to fix what's already broken, Liv? What can you do to restore my trust in your words? Because I truly do not trust you anymore. And that, right there, is the problem. I can't be friends with someone I can't trust."

"I'll find a way. I promise."

Ava did not answer, and Olivia didn't know what to add to that.

Their conversation ended with a heavy silence, and the only sound was the both of them breaking down for different reasons.

CHAPTER 12

OLIVIA

Three days after Olivia had spoken to Ava, an idea struck her.

Her father seized all her social media accounts, so she knew she couldn't use those. Not that she didn't try. Locked out, probably because her father had changed her passwords as an extra measure to have her not address this whole scandal.

But just like with any kid with strict parents, Olivia had options—a burner account she used for close and trusted friends. In this case, she was followed by her brothers, Ava, and another girl she starred in a movie with way back when. It wasn't enough to get her the attention she needed, but it was enough of a start. So, at Nikos' guidance, she used his phone, plus his office where the WiFi and network weren't cut off, and put her plan in motion.

First, she had to follow a few people. She started by making her Instagram profile public and decided that she would leave up the images she had been sharing on the account. These were so unlike the public image people were used to seeing of her, so she knew they would get her the attention she needed. They were all selfies and very random in a way that screamed "human." They were not the coordinated nightmare that was her "official" account.

The next thing she did was follow a few gossip sites she knew that were all about breaking the "next big Hollywood story." She followed about ten accounts before she got notified that someone had followed her. And then, a few more followers came in and she knew she had the attention she needed.

Then, her real plan started.

She was going live.

"Hello, world," she started, already having ten people on her stream. "My name is Olivia Clarke. I need to talk about something important, something that has been eating away at me for a while now." And then, she started addressing the rumors like she had wanted to for the longest time.

She spoke about that night when the scandal happened. What had pushed her to say what she did, why she did the things she did, how much she betrayed her best friend, and also addressed the speculations about her that had come up along the way. She'd had to write it all out after spending a few hours searching the internet and reading as much of the gossip that was circulating about her as she could stomach.

No, she wasn't on drugs. She certainly was not pregnant, nor was she in rehab. She spent more time addressing Ava and clarified that, at no point during their night, had Ava drugged her or forced her to do any drugs of any kind.

She didn't dare look at the number of people watching her live because she knew she would chicken out.

"I feel trapped, you see," Ava said, reaching the tail end of everything she wanted to address. "I want to be the best person I can be for myself and the people I love, but it's hard when I'm not being authentic." The comments section was buzzing, but Olivia pressed on, intent on ignoring everything and everyone. "I've spent a lot of time hiding behind a persona, projecting an image of myself that wasn't entirely true because that is what's expected of me.

I've been living a version of myself that fit into the expectations of others. But, in doing so, I've lost touch with who I truly am. I was afraid of showing my flaws, afraid of being rejected for who I really am."

"I want to change that," Olivia continued, her voice shaking. "I want to be honest about who I am and who I want to become. And that starts with speaking my truth, letting you all know what happened, and how I plan to move forward. I've been living in fear of disappointing everyone, of not meeting the standards set by society or the people around me, but all I've ended up with is being a disappointment to myself. And, in that fear, I sacrificed my authenticity too. It's exhausting trying to be someone you're not," she concluded, shaking her head. "But, I'm done with that. I want to break free from this trap and embrace who I truly am, flaws and all. It's just so damn hard when you've built a façade for so long. But I need to do it for myself, for my sanity, and for the relationships that matter to me."

"To Ava, and to everyone hurt by my words and actions. I can't change the past, but I can promise you I'm committed to being better. I hope you can find it in your hearts to forgive me." She stopped, not knowing if she should say this or not, but decided she just as well might. "I miss you, Ava, and I want a chance to make things right. You are my world and I'm sorry I've been such a rotten friend to you. I hope we can mend what's broken between us, because I need you. I *love* you."

With a heavy sigh, her eyes wandered to the top of the screen to check how many people were tuned in. Olivia balked at the number, but thankfully she was done since all her confidence chose that moment to vanish. She quickly ended the live stream, and all but threw the phone she had borrowed face down onto the table.

2.5 million people! 2.5 million people had tuned in? What the hell?!

At the very least, she had expected about two hundred. Her neck and armpits itched as nerves overtook her, but, thankfully, she was done.

"How did it go?" Nikos asked Olivia some time later.

It was early evening and they, once again, found themselves in each other's company. It had become such a routine source of comfort that

Olivia didn't know she was missing him until he found her in the music room, where she was playing on the piano.

"I don't know," she shrugged, as she stopped and stood to look at him. "I'm too afraid to look." Nikos enveloped her in a hug and then kissed her. He had started doing that a few days ago and, if she was being honest with herself, she didn't hate it. Not even a little bit. "How did your thing go?"

He'd told her about his last conversation with his grandfather and how much he wanted to make the man trust that he wasn't going to sell their hotel anymore. "Not as well as I would have wanted to. I think it's going to take some time."

"I hear you," Olivia said. "I think my thing will also take some time. But I'm glad I finally addressed it."

"Yeah?"

"Yes. I feel like this heavy burden I've been carrying around was suddenly lifted and I can breathe much better."

"Have you spoken to your dad?"

"Not yet. He called, though. I've been dodging Iossif for most of the day."

Nikos laughed, which made her smile. "Tell you what, why don't we shake off this day? I don't know

about you, but I could use a break right about now."
Nikos suggested, an excited twinkle in his eyes.

"Sounds like a plan," Olivia said, appreciating
the opportunity to not think about what the world
had to say about her confession, if Ava had watched
it, and also not wanting to know what her father
had to say. Maybe in a few days, she'd have enough
courage to do so, but not today.

"Let's go swimming," he suggested.

CHAPTER 13
OLIVIA

"I can't believe you don't know how to swim," Olivia said with a delightful giggle.

"I can float," Nikos responded. "That's pretty much the same thing."

"That is *so* not the same thing!"

"Why not?" Nikos asked as he stood waist-deep in the water.

"Because you can't do this," Olivia declared, showcasing her swimming skills by effortlessly swimming laps around him. She moved through the water with grace and confidence, well aware of how intently Nikos was watching her. And, maybe, she might have been showing off a little bit.

"Okay, that was impressive," Nikos said when she came back up for air. He pulled her to him so they were standing chest to chest. "You are impressive."

"I can teach you," she said, not sure what to say to that.

Not for the first time, she wondered what the hell was happening between the two of them. Ever since the night they went out to the beach, he's been... affectionate. He randomly gave her hugs and kisses and even made her food. Every morning, before he'd left to run his business, he'd made her breakfast and waited until she woke up and finished eating before he left. A few times, she'd intentionally been late to breakfast to see what he would do, and every time, he had waited for her.

"Or we can do this." He then leaned down and kissed her.

His kiss was slow and sensual. He kissed her like he was savoring the moment, his arms wrapping more around her as he pulled her body flash to his.

The sun had dipped lower on the horizon and they were the only ones crazy enough to still be out in the sea. However, this afforded them the privacy that made it feel like it was just the two of them around, notwithstanding the other guests at the hotel.

Nikos' body was warm and hard muscles against

her soft curves. Not even the chilly breeze brought on by the sea penetrated the warmth she found herself cocooned between his hands.

A tiny moan left Olivia when Nikos bit her lip, making her press harder into him and pull him lower. He responded by lifting her until her legs wrapped around his waist. At this angle, their kiss went even harder and got deeper until Olivia pulled back to take in some much-needed air.

Nikos didn't stop, though. His lips moved down, caressing her neck and gently kissing the sensitive area where her neck met her shoulders. A shudder rocked her body as her head fell back. He held her hair to hold her head in place and then bit down, sucking at the spot he had been kissing.

Olivia groaned as she ground herself on Nikos' hard warm body, wanting to feel everything he could give her, but, in the back of her mind, was a nagging thought. *What were they doing?*

Sure, it felt good that she badly wanted it to be real, but they had yet to talk about whatever was developing between them. He made her feel things she hadn't felt with anyone before, and it scared her a little.

Okay... it was a lot more than a little, but she refused to acknowledge it, otherwise, she might overthink.

Maybe her thoughts translated into her body language because Nikos pulled back and asked, "What's wrong?" He searched her face, a frown marring his face.

"Nothing," Olivia said as she shook herself off, then pulled away from him, jumping back into the water. "It's getting cold. We should get back."

"Wait," he grabbed at her before she swam away. "Talk to me." The words were right at the tip of her tongue, but how to say them without sounding like a whiny, clingy little girl with her first crush? "Is it something I did?"

"Do you think this, what's happening between us, is just a comfort thing?" She decided to just throw it out there because she didn't want this to spiral. It was best to find out now where they stand rather than later.

"What?" Nikos asked as she finally turned back to look at him.

"This," she gestured between them. "It started because we both needed an escape. And I can't help but think that it's going to fizzle out as fast as it started."

"Yes, it started out as a comfort thing," he said, and her stomach tightened. "But it's a lot more than that for me now." *Really?* She wanted to say but didn't. She instead searched his eyes, trying to tell if he was speaking the truth or not. Olivia held her breath, waiting for him to continue. And the way everything else but them faded away made it feel like everything around them was also holding its breath as she waited for his next words. "I like you, Olivia. I have for a while."

There was a softness in his gaze that had her releasing the breath she didn't know she'd been holding. The sincerity in his words resonated in the gentle breeze by the beach as the world around them picked up once again.

"This, what's happening between us, is quite new to me. I find you intriguing and you challenge me, Olivia," he continued. "You've helped in the past few days in more ways than you will ever know. But, it's a lot more than just helping me. I want to explore this. To explore *us* and who we are outside the problems that brought us together."

"I like you too," Olivia confessed. "I just..."

"Wish we had met under different circumstances?" he asked as he searched her face.

"Yes." That's exactly what she was thinking. *How easy would it have been if they had met on a date versus at a runaway hotel where she was hiding like the little coward she was?*

"True connections aren't bound by circumstances."

"What?"

"That's something my dad told me once," Nikos said as he smiled. "He was a firm believer that everything that happened to us and that everyone we met was by design, no matter the circumstances that made it happen."

"Do you believe the same?" she challenged.

"I believe I needed your help to make the right decision about the Atlantis." She gave him a skeptical look. "No, think about it," he let out a short laugh. "If you hadn't been living with me, we wouldn't have had the chance to meet. It's only because we met, we went out that night, and you were vulnerable with me. After that, I was vulnerable enough to open up about the hotel. If I didn't tell you, you wouldn't have taken me on that tour and reminded me why I loved it. And I certainly would have messed up my relationship with *Papous*. So, you see, Liv, me and you, we were exactly where we needed to be when we found each other."

"Our destiny, huh?" It sounded absurd, and yet, the more she thought about it, the more it made sense. She certainly would have still been drowning in pity if it wasn't for Nikos, as she had been more than happy to hide away in the hotel and away from everyone.

"I think it's beautiful how we met. I wouldn't change it for anything else." He took her hand. "This is a lot more than just a comfort thing. And I really, *really* want to explore this with you. Will you allow me? Allow us?"

"Take me on a date first, then we'll see," Olivia joked, not knowing what to say.

"Done!" Nikos responded without hesitation, surprising her.

"Are you going to get out of the car?" Nikos asked as he tapped on the window.

True to his words, he had taken her on a date. That very night, when she had asked him. Within two hours, they were at some place Nikos said she would love.

"I was waiting for you to open my door," Olivia said, hoping her voice was light enough to cover up the nerves that suddenly assaulted her.

It was one thing to think about going on a date; it was another for Nikos to actually take her. She tried to remember the last time she had gone on a date and all that came up were memories of dates set up by her father and the PR team as a publicity stunt. They always made sure she had a script, knew what to say, and how to act.

Here, she was on a date with Nikos with no idea of how to do either. It's why she had not opened her door, because all her dates were scripted for the man to open her door and treat her as much as a princess as possible. The absence of the script now left her at a loss as she grappled with the unfamiliarity of the situation.

She badly wanted to make a good impression on Nikos since they were officially on their first date, but not knowing how to act made her feel well out of her element—even though she tried to act otherwise. However, the clamminess in her hands and the air in her stomach betrayed the nerves that danced beneath the calm exterior she was projecting.

"Of course," Nikos said as he opened the door and extended his hand out to her. "Can I have your hand, princess?"

Of course, he meant it as a joke because he couldn't have known the internal monologue going on with her, but it slighted her just a little bit that he called her princess. It tapped into the insecurities that this short moment had unveiled.

She had to brush it off though, intent on having a good night on her unofficial first date, so with a gracious award-winning smile, she gave him her hand as he helped her out.

"Thank you," she said, making her tone light as she tapped into her vast experience of faking it till you make it. *She was an actress, after all.*

They were seated as soon as they entered. The way people around them rushed and fussed around Nikos reminded her he was. indeed. A well-known individual on the island. She had noticed it every time they were around people, but Nikos seemed oblivious to it, mostly because he usually had all his attention on her.

They sat in a quiet part of the restaurant, hidden away from the main area enough to give privacy, but not so much that it was isolated. A soft ambient glow illuminated the room, coming from strategically placed pendant lights suspended from the exposed wooden beams above them. Bathed in a warm, intimate atmosphere that added a touch of romance to the place. Soft music came from somewhere, but she wasn't bothered enough to find out.

"You look beautiful tonight." She turned around to find Nikos giving her such an intense look that she had to look away. Her flaming face was the only indicator the unexpected compliment affected her.

"Liv," he said, his fingers gently turning her face until she was looking at him again, "you look beautiful."

His voice was gentle and his fingers rubbed her face with feather-like touches, and yet, they left a zing of electricity that traveled all across her body, leaving her feeling very much awake.

"Thank you," she whispered as the heat in her face traveled to the back of her head and down her chest. She might look as bright as a tomato right now, and her red hair did nothing to help. *That was just embarrassing.*

Thankfully, the server chose that moment to interrupt them and ask for their orders. The intrusion gave her a brief respite from the intense gaze Nikos had been directing toward her.

Once again, Olivia was reminded that she didn't have the script she always depended on to tell her what she should get. A moment of panic seized her as she scanned the menu, the unfamiliarity of the menu items making her feel a bit adrift.

"We'll have the chef's special, plus a bottle of your finest wine," Nikos said when Olivia did not respond to the numerous questions the server asked her. And now she couldn't look at Nikos. She couldn't bear the idea that she'd look up and see disgust at her incompetence to function like a normal person would. It was days like this one when she was reminded just how much control her father had taken over her life when she could barely function in social gatherings without being told what to do. "Are you okay?" Nikos asked her as he tried to get her to look at him.

"Peachy," she responded, fidgeting with the tablecloth, folding and unfolding it.

"I can't help if you don't tell me what the problem is," he insisted as he grabbed her hands so she had no excuse but to look up at him.

Olivia had always prided herself on honesty and, immediately, she decided it was best to tell him the issue now before things went further for them. So, she confessed about how her previous dates had always been scripted for her, from what she would say and eat, right down to the clothes she wore and how she smelled.

Saying it out loud made her feel very juvenile and like she was a child. As if she were admitting to a habit, she should have outgrown.

She braced herself for Nikos' reaction, unsure of how he would perceive this glimpse into the very restricted life. "Is that why it took you almost an hour to decide what dress to wear?" he asked instead, surprising her.

Olivia blinked up at him in confusion, before a small smile that mirrored his own tugged at the corner of her lips. "Well, yes. I had to find just the perfect dress." And then insecurity rolled in. "Is it not good?"

She ended up wearing a little black strapless dress that hugged her in all the right places. She would have loved to wear heels with it to accentuate her legs, but settled for the white sneakers she had when she landed. They were the only decent pair of shoes she'd brought with her. Her dress was barely decent, but it wasn't pajamas or a sundress, so it had to do.

Maybe she should have gone shopping first?

"It's perfect," Nikos responded, effectively pausing her inner rumblings.

She was still waiting for him to judge her based on what she'd revealed, but he brushed it off like it was not something to worry about. "Why?" she asked him, unable to help herself.

"Why is your dress perfect?" He frowned as he looked down at the parts of the dress he could see over the table. "Well, I guess—"

"Why are you not freaking out about what I said about my scripted life?" She cut him off. The air she'd had in her stomach had made a steady return.

Nikos leaned back in his chair, studying her for a moment, and a soft smile gracing his lips. "Liv, I can't claim to know anything about your life or even how Hollywood runs. All I know is that you shared something intimate with me, which shows that you trust me enough to let your guard down around me. I appreciate that more than you know. And as for the scripted life, all I know is that this," he gestured between them, "is unscripted. The real you is sitting across from me right now, and that's the woman I want to get to know. We'll deal with everything else later, when it comes up."

Olivia didn't know what to say to that. Once their food arrived, she didn't have to because Nikos excitedly invited her to dig in as he told her about what she was eating and challenged her to tell him the ingredients she was tasting for the different plates of food he had ordered.

By the time their food was done, she had forgotten her worries about what to say and do as Nikos' enthusiasm and charisma invited her to do and say whatever felt right. Like a gentleman, he helped her off her chair when it was time to go home, and then into and out of the car.

However, unlike a gentleman, right after kissing her good night and "ending" their first date, Nikos got on his knees in front of her and pulled her to him until he stood right between her opened thighs.

"Nikos!" She gasped at the sudden movements, pushing her hands out so she could catch herself on his shoulders.

"I've wanted to do this since we went swimming," he mumbled, and without warning, he pulled her panties off and went straight for her clit, rolling it between his warm lips.

A strong shudder racked Olivia's body as she fell back, releasing a rough moan. The door thankfully held her in place and Nikos' powerful hold on her thighs. He shifted them so she was straddling his face completely, leaving her at his mercy, and then dove into her center with gusto, sucking and licking her like it was the last thing he'll ever do.

"Fuck Nikos," Olivia trembled. Her limbs were feeling as light as they were tight to a point where she couldn't feel anything more than the lips that were licking up her wetness and giving her the most intense pleasure. Her nipples stood at attention, and she had an incredible urge to pinch them to release some pressure. But, she couldn't find it in herself to let go of the hold she had on Nikos' face as she ground herself on him.

He chose that moment to stand but didn't dislodge them, so now Olivia was suspended in the air, on his shoulders. It was incredibly hot.

She chanced a look down at him to find Nikos already looking up at her. What made the scene hotter was the view of his tongue moving up and down as he licked her senseless.

"Mind your head," he mumbled. Then, they were moving, and his tongue was right back where she needed it.

The next time she was aware of her surroundings, Olivia was lying on the bed and Nikos was ripping the little dress off her body. He threw it somewhere behind him, his eyes never leaving her body. "Magnificent," he rasped, his voice many octaves deeper than it usually was. He shed his clothes at lightning speed and then he was over her once again. "I'm going to go very first," Nikos warned as he lined his length right where she needed him. "And then, when we've both come and I've taken the edge off, I'll make love to you. Is that okay?"

She had barely moaned out a yes before Nikos

was inside and moving so fast that they started moving up the bed. "Oh, baby, you feel so good," Nikos said as he leaned down so their bodies molded together.

He took her head in his hands and kissed her, then moved so his legs were under her ass. This position gave him leverage to hold her in place as he went in even deeper.

"Nikos, I can't hold off," Olivia moaned, her insides clenching at an oncoming orgasm.

"Cum for me, baby," he demanded as his pace increased even more. When his hand snaked between them and started rubbing her clit, Olivia couldn't back anymore. Her orgasm was so intense that she blacked out for a hot minute with pleasure, so intense that it was painful and racked her body. The only thing that penetrated her haze was the sound of Nikos cumming and the tightness she felt as his fingers dug into her sides. By the time she was fully aware of her surroundings, he had her in the bathroom and was slowly washing her body. "There she is." Nikos smiled down at her.

"That was... intense," Olivia said as her body sagged. It was more from the intense orgasm than being tired.

"Our night had just begun," he whispered in her

ear before running his hands through her hair and washing it out.

And it was true, if his hard length rubbing her back as he washed her was anything to go by. By the end of the night, Olivia was riding such a high that she felt like she was on drugs.

This high took her into the next morning, but it quickly came crashing down when she found her dad and brothers in her kitchen, helping themselves to the coffee she had come down to make.

CHAPTER 14
OLIVIA

"What the hell?" Olivia screamed and rushed back out of the room.

"Pause," her father barked out, stopping her in her tracks. Her father's voice was the final straw as she came back to reality, like a bucket of ice water poured over her.

"Dad! Hello. Good morning," she said in a falsetto, going for nonchalance but failing miserably.

Her brothers, Zayn and Jax, snickered behind their father.

"I told you to not say anything. Didn't I say that?" Her father asked in a very calm-before-the-storm kind of voice. She was very familiar with this tone because it's one where he ended up blowing up so much it took the sheer strength of willpower to make it through talking to him.

"You mentioned something like that, yes," she said as she resigned to her fate by moving into the kitchen and taking a seat next to Jax.

Jax and Zayn were twin heartthrobs and a favorite in Hollywood. Unlike her, though, they had the autonomy their father could not allow her, especially since their mother passed.

Jax wore black on black with a touch of eyeliner highlighting his dark green eyes. His red hair combed back and held in place by hairpins. He wore rings and earrings that always made him stand out. On the other hand, Zayn was wearing all bright colors, in the stereotypical vacation shirt and shorts, which was made even more ridiculous by the lime green band he had around his red hair. Everything her brothers did was to rebel against what their father wanted, so she had no doubt that this was what it was right now. Although, she couldn't tell sometimes if what they did was to rebel or if it was simply something they wanted to do.

In contrast, their father wore a pressed suit, probably custom-made, right down to his name-brand shoes. His dark hair cropped short on his head and his green eyes, much like his children's, glared at her with the intensity of all the suns.

"My exact words," her father started, "were do not, under any circumstance, address this bullshit. Did I not say that?"

"Not in those exact words," she grumbled, but stopped at the glare her father sent her.

"Do you know what you just did? The mess your little charade caused?"

"By mess, he means that the heat is on him now," Jax said in a bored tone that was very reminiscent of the same tone their father adapted when he was dismissive.

"Hey, stay out of this," their dad glared at Jax. "Olivia will fix—"

"There is nothing to fix, Pops," Zayn cut in as he poured himself a second cup of coffee. "Aren't you the one who always says 'we shouldn't address the rumors'?" He deepened his voice to quote their father's usage of that sentence every time rumors came up about the family.

Except this was of their own making. Olivia wasn't sure that same argument stood. She wasn't sure what people were saying and, based on her father's reaction and the fact that he was here, it couldn't have been good.

And yet, she didn't feel bad about what she did. At least not as much as she should have.

"It will go away," Jax added in a tone Olivia knew was mocking their father. She wanted to laugh at this turn of the tables, but one look at their father's red face and glare at her brothers let her know she should keep her comments to herself. "Besides, I think Liv here did good," Jax added, sending a proud smile her way as he squeezed her shoulder.

"Did good? Her little video is dragging our family name through the mud!"

"Typical Dad," Zayn tsked. "More worried about what other people have to say than what his children have to say. Did you even watch the video, or did you stupid publicist give you cliff-notes?"

"Watch yourself," their dad warned, glaring at Zayn.

"No, you watch yourself, Dad!" Zayn said as he squared up to their father. "You don't get to come here and throw blame without acknowledging the part you had to play in this whole thing."

"Your publicist is the one to blame for this clusterfuck. And, just like we thought, you are blaming our little sister for this. We won't let you. You want to fix this mess? How about hiring a better publicist for starters? And, maybe, be a better father?"

"You will not lecture me on what to do, young man," their father all but shouted. It never really took much to set him off, especially when it came to his sons. Of course, at this point, her brothers were now squaring up and glaring at their dad with the same intensity he was giving them.

Olivia had forgotten that, as much as her father pushed her buttons, no one knew how to push his like his sons did. They never knew how to have an amicable conversation. *Case in point.* But she was glad her brothers had come because it would have been a hell of a lot harder to deal with him on her own.

"Well, someone has to!" Jax threw his hands up. "You have forgotten what it's like to be a father ever since Mom—"

"Whoa, whoa, whoa!" came a random voice, interrupting what Olivia knew Jax was going to say. "What's going on here? What's with all the yelling?"

Oh, dear heavens! Olivia had all but forgotten that Nikos was still in the house!

"Who the fuck are you?" Jax and Zayn asked in the same annoyed tone.

"What are you doing here?" their dad asked.

"Nikos!" Olivia gasped.

"You know this man?" Jax and Zayn asked once again, turning simultaneously to look at her.

"Stop that!" She shuddered at their in-sync twin thing that they usually fell into.

"Liv? Are you okay?" Nikos rushed to her side, ignoring all the other Clarkes in the room.

"I'm fine," she smiled up at him despite herself.

He cradled her face in that manner he liked to do. "Are you sure? Do you need backup?"

"Back up?"

"What the fuck?" she heard her brothers say, but she ignored them.

"I'm good." Olivia smiled. "You're dressed. Are you going somewhere?"

"Yes. *Papous* needs me to run some errands. Are you sure you're okay?"

"I will be." Olivia couldn't help but smile.

Nikos searched her eyes with a mix of concern and genuine care. His fingers gently traced her cheek, as if trying to read the emotions etched on her face. She was well-aware of the incredulous looks she was getting, but she wanted to exist in the brief moment of relief Nikos' presence had provided.

"If you need anything, just let me know. I'm here for you," he reassured her.

"I know, and thank you. I'll be okay. Just take care of whatever your *Papous* needs. I'll take care of my family."

Nikos nodded in understanding, then leaned in, kissed, and hugged her. That time, she could *not* ignore the bewilderment in the room. Olivia reluctantly pulled away and chanced a look around the room. Her brothers were rightfully confused, but their father was now glaring daggers at Nikos.

With one final reassuring smile, Nikos turned around and acknowledged her family like he didn't just shock them with their actions. Then he headed outside, throwing one last look at Olivia. She couldn't help but notice the protective glint in his eyes. It brought butterflies to her stomach despite herself.

"Dad," Olivia began as a way to explain the situation, but also draw her father's glare from being directed at Nikos. "That was—"

"Absolutely not!"

"You didn't even let me explain." *Of course, he wouldn't.*

"I understand perfectly what's happening and I reject it," her father declared firmly, crossing his arms.

"I'm sorry, you reject *it*? Reject what, exactly?"

Olivia questioned, her eyebrows furrowed in barely concealed anger.

"This," he waved at her, then waved when Nikos went out of the room, "whatever is going on with *that* man."

"I like him," she glared up at her father.

"You'll have someone better," he responded dismissively, like that was the end of the conversation.

"You mean, someone that *you* picked out for me?" Olivia wouldn't let it go as she matched his stand.

"Yes," he responded like it was a no-brainer.

Olivia scoffed right in sync with her brothers, this time at the ridiculousness of their father's statement.

"Do you even hear the words coming out of your mouth sometimes?" Zayn asked. "Like, do you actually listen to yourself?"

Their father glared at Zayn. "First of all, I did not authorize that relationship," he pointed at where Olivia and Nikos had been standing just moments before. "Second, we have a plan to turn all this unneeded attention around—"

"Un-needed because the attention is on you now?" Olivia interrupted.

"*And*," their father continued like she had said nothing, "it involves you being in a very public relationship with a celebrity of your caliber. Not some nobody."

"Since when did our lives become some publicity stunt?" Jax interrupted, pinning their father with a glare. "You have your head so far up your ass that you don't even recognize what you are doing to your own children."

"I've had enough of the two of you!" If they had neighbors, they would definitely have called the police now because their father shouted so hard he could have blown off the roof. "This has nothing to do with you," he glared at Jax and Zayn.

"Oh, but it does. It is, after all, our family name we need to protect. That's all you care about, isn't it, Pops? Not the fact that you'd rather have your child sad and miserable to protect the family name rather than see her happy with someone that she might actually like?"

"We all have roles to play. And if it involves a few unfortunate relationships, so be it."

"What about what we want, Dad?" Olivia spoke up before her brothers could jump in. "What about our happiness? Does that ever factor in with these plans and roles you would have us play?"

"No, he'd rather win public favor than think about that. Right, Dad?" Jax's tone was mocking and did the opposite of what Olivia had wanted. "I mean, screw having a functional family. Who cares about that when the public loves you, right?"

They ended up yelling and shouting at each other to the point Olivia just faded into the background and let it happen. Her brothers were intent on saying as many hurtful things as they could while their father played the "I'm the adult, you must obey me" card. Of course, Jax and Zayn were so against being told what to do that had only encouraged them further until their father left.

"Do you have to goad him so much?" Olivia sighed once they heard the door close with a loud bang.

"Until he learns, we are people with feelings and not property to do with as he pleases, I'm afraid so." Jax took a seat next to her.

"Besides, you don't do it enough. You let him get away with far too much." Zayn added.

"I'd rather maintain the peace."

"Exactly," they said at the same time.

"God, I hate when you do that." They sat in silence for a while and Olivia was lost in thought. Her brothers and father had differing opinions on her video, and she wondered if it was the same with the public. *What did Ava think?* Of course, this did not encourage her to check out the feedback. If anything, she had decided that she would *not* check them out. But she had to know. "How is Ava?"

"It's going to take some time, Liv," Jax responded. "Her family took a lot of damage."

That much had been obvious to her based on her last conversation with Olivia.

"Not to worry, she will bounce back in no time. That Ava Reid is feisty." Zayn said, and she turned to see him with a goofy faraway look on his face he always got when talking about her best friend.

"Hey!" Jax slapped the back of his head. "Stop that."

"Stop what?" Zayn asked, as he rubbed his head while glaring at his twin.

"That stupid look. I know what you're thinking."

"I wasn't—"

"I would rather not know what you are thinking about my best friend," Olivia held a hand up to stop Zayn.

"What I want to know is who was that tall glass of water?" Jax asked, now wearing the goofy look his twin had.

Zayn scoffed while Olivia said, "His name is Nikos and he's off-limits to you."

"I THOUGHT YOU HAD LEFT."

Olivia and her brothers had spoken some more about Nikos, her video, and their father before she'd checked if he was still around many hours later.

It had taken her a while, but she finally found him by the beach in a semi-secluded area. His tie and jacket were off and he looked deep in thought, so her presence had surprised him.

"I couldn't reach my driver," he said, holding up his phone.

Olivia braced for his confrontational mood; he seemed to adapt when he interacted with his children. When it didn't come, she sat close to him in the hot sand. "There's no network here."

"I remembered," her dad laughed. Olivia mustered up the energy to crack a smile, but it was barely there. This was already weird, and they hadn't even exchanged three words. "I watched the video you made," her father said, surprising her. "Do you really feel like you're caged?"

"Yes," she responded in a tiny voice as she peered up at him, not wanting to set him off.

"Explain it to me," her father requested, slightly turning his torso to look down at her.

"Really?" Olivia raised a skeptical eyebrow, trying to gauge what her father was playing at.

"Really. Your brothers said some... things. And then, you said some things in your video. I simply want to understand."

"I don't like acting," Olivia started there, feeling the soft sand beneath her feet as a distraction.

"*Really*?" her father responded in surprise. "I thought acting was your dream." He slid the sunglasses that were on his head over his eyes to cover them, probably to shield him from the sun as he glanced around the landscape.

Olivia did not grab a pair, instead using her hand as a shield when she looked up at her father.

"It was when I was a child and had zero interests. I haven't wanted to be in any more movies since we shot the musical. I told you this." A gentle sea breeze ruffled her hair, and she welcomed the gentle respite from the burning heat.

"I thought you didn't want to be in musicals anymore? That's why I didn't accept any scripts that are musicals."

"No, Dad. I said *movies*. I thought you understood, but then you came to me with a new script every day after that I gave up on telling you this wasn't my dream."

"Why didn't you tell me?" He sounded frustrated, and Olivia couldn't tell if he was being funny.

"Because I never see you unless you're telling me what to do." Half the time, she interacted with him through their publicist.

"Right." He grew quiet, making her wonder what was going on in his mind. "What do you like then?" he asked, eventually.

"I like to sing."

"You do?"

"Why are you surprised?"

"Because you said you don't like acting in musicals. It makes no sense."

"Dad, two things can be true. I can love singing without being in musicals," she laughed, a seashell crunching underfoot as she shifted in the sand.

He looked bewildered. "I feel like I don't know who my children are anymore."

"Because you don't." She wanted to say that gently, but there really was no easy way to tell someone they are a bad parent.

"Your mother was always the better one out of both of us." He smiled sadly.

"You are too. Or, at least, you used to be. But, it's like ever since mom died, you haven't cared about anything but what *she* wanted. And that has blinded you to what we actually want. Dad, you can't keep pleasing her because Mom's not here anymore. We are."

"I care about what you want," he sounded offended.

"You care about what *you* think I want. What you think we *should* want."

"Do your brothers feel the same way?" he asked after a brief pause.

"Jax wants to be a jeweler," Olivia gave her father a reality check. "Every piece of jewelry he wears, he's made on his own. Zayn is interested in studying forensics science. But I bet you didn't know that." Of course, he didn't—going by his dropped jaw and bewildered look on his face. "Dad, to you, I'm supposed to be your obedient little girl who plays her role to a tee. You never give me a chance to react to anything because you already have everything mapped out for me. You don't have control over the twins, so you push all responsibility on me."

This had always been a place of contention for them. She hated him most days for it, and yet, she loved him too because he was her father. It was a very disturbing feeling that never truly sat right with her.

"Your grandfather said that we needed an agent to keep the family in line. That's all I've been doing since Mom died. I'm trying to do as good a job as she would have done to keep everything in place." He looked down at her like he hoped she would understand, but it was hard for Olivia to understand any of her father's past actions—not when her heart felt heavy and her throat burned as she held back her true feelings.

"I get that. You are trying your best. But, Dad," her voice wobbled, "we don't need an agent. We need our dad. It's hard enough not having Mom, but it's like we lost you as soon as we lost her."

Olivia's words hung in the air between them as they both turned around to look at the waves gently clashing with the bank. It had been a long time since Olivia had a heart-to-heart with her father, or even just sat down and spoken to him, that she was exhausted from releasing years of resentment and frustrations in only a few words.

She had always imagined she would scream

these words out to get him to understand, but she didn't have to. Although she didn't find the peace she thought she'd get when she laid herself bare.

"I've been so focused on keeping things together that I didn't realize I was drifting away from the ones who needed me the most," he admitted, a mix of regret and vulnerability in his voice.

Olivia didn't know if it had been her words, what her brothers had said, the video she had made, or maybe a combination of different things, but something had finally pierced the hard shell their father had built up. It looked like he was coming off the high he'd been riding on for years.

She was not about to question why or what it was, but all she could remember in this moment was Nikos' words: *True connections aren't bound by circumstances.*

CHAPTER 15

OLIVIA

"Is Dad... smiling?" Jax asked as they watched their father in the kitchen.

"And cooking?" Zayn was equally bewildered.

So was Olivia.

Nikos' grandmother, who had asked them to call her *Yiayia*, had invited them for dinner the day before they were all leaving the island.

Ever since her heart-to-heart with their father three days ago, Zayn, Jax, and Olivia had been looking at him like he sprouted a second head. But, it was Zayn and Jax mostly, since Olivia was a little aware of the change in their father since her talk with him. She hadn't shared what was said with her brothers because she believed that their father should be the one to bridge the gap between them. However, she hadn't expected to see him so unlike himself.

"Why are we standing here?" Nikos whispered next to Olivia.

They had all come to a synchronized stop when they got to *Yiayia's* kitchen and found their dad smiling like he was Jolly Old Saint Nicholas himself.

"Do you see this?" Jax whisper-shouted in response as he wildly gestured to the scene before them.

"My *Yiayia* is cooking with your father?" Nikos asked, confused.

"Exactly!" all three responded.

He held his hands up in surrender, probably because the Clarke siblings were glaring at him as if he should know better. Nikos then made his way further into the kitchen, leaving them standing where they were.

"Can you believe this?" *Papous* said as he entered the house from the backdoor. "I come into the kitchen and she kicks me out. He comes in and, suddenly, she had no problem cooking with someone else?"

Papous had his back to them as he complained to

Nikos. Olivia shared a look with Jax and Zayn, who both looked like they were just about ready to leave.

"Do you think if we move back slowly, they'll know we left?" Zayn whispered conspiratorially.

"We can try," Olivia said to humor him.

"But, I'm hungry. I haven't had a home cooked meal in a while," Jax said.

Olivia admitted that a home cooked meal trumped the weirdness of the moment right now. The scent of delicious food and baked goods wafted in the air in a way that was inviting.

Just as they decided to stay, *Yiayia* noticed them.

"Why are you just standing there? Come, join us," she rushed to them, then turned to her husband and said something in Greek.

Papous rolled his eyes but got up, slightly dragging Nikos with him out of the room.

The room was filled with the clattering of pots and pans, the sizzle of ingredients meeting a hot pan as their father flipped something. They approached where Nikos and *Papous* had just vacated the seats and sat down.

Yiayia turned around and spoke Greek to their dad, who, to their surprise, responded in perfect Greek.

"You speak Greek?" Zayn asked for them.

"I speak a lot of languages," their dad laughed before turning back to whatever they were making.

"Your father here is quite exceptional," *Yiayia* said.

"Oh, stop with the frowns," their dad laughed when he turned back to them. "There is a lot about me you guys don't know."

"Evidently," Olivia said as they watched him shift his attention to whatever was in the oven.

"He taught my Constantine how to speak English, and Constantine taught him Greek."

"It was a nightmare for us all," *Papous* said as he returned with Nikos, both holding boxes in their hands.

"Oh, come on, we weren't that bad," their dad protested.

"Tell that to the house you burned down," *Yiayia* responded as she moved to another pot on the stove.

And then, back and forth, Olivia's dad, *Papous*, and *Yiayia* continued to reminisce about his childhood with Constantine, who was *Yiayia* and *Papous'* late son.

The Clarke siblings watched in a mixture of comic disbelief and bewilderment as they saw a version of their dad they had never met before. They occasionally shared looks as if confirming with each other that they were looking at the same thing.

At some point, Nikos stole Olivia away, but only after they had eaten all the sweets *Yiayia* insisted on feeding them. They would have had more if Papous had not objected to going back to fetch more boxes.

"I have never seen my father like that. I think we are all pretty freaked out," she said as soon as they were away from the noise in the kitchen.

"I think *Yiayia* and *Papous* are excited to have more company," Nikos said as he put an arm around her.

They headed toward the beach in the late evening.

"It's been ages since I saw my dad smile that hard," Olivia admitted. "It's weird. Like seeing a turtle out of its shell."

Nikos burst out in laughter. "That's a very weird way of putting it."

"It is *that* weird," she chuckled.

"To be honest, I don't think *Papous* and *Yiayia* have been that animated before. At least, as much as I remember," he said after sobering. "Maybe it had something to do with your dad."

"My dad? Why?" Olivia stopped walking, prompting Nikos to follow suit.

"Well, he lived at the hotel for a while with my dad," he said. "I think it feels like they got back a piece of their son through your dad. Is that weird?"

"That's not weird at all," she responded, a thoughtful expression on her face. "Although, now I'm seeing what you meant by your fate mumbo jumbo."

"Mumbo jumbo?" he leaned back, feigning shock.

"You know what I mean," Olivia shrugged, shoving him gently.

"It's strange how life works, isn't it? Your dad knew my dad, and now, here, you and I are, continuing the family cycle. Who knew?"

"I'm grateful for how this turned out."

"Me too," he pulled her into his arms. "I hope you are ready for my crazy family, Olivia Clarke, because I'm never letting you go."

"Well, I come with an overbearing family and a whole lot of public opinions. Last chance to back out."

"No chance, baby."

"No take backs," Olivia smiled as Nikos leaned in and kissed her.

To see the list of books for Dawn Baca

www.dawnbaca.com/books

Newsletter

www.dawnbaca.com/blog

Also by Dawn Baca

Women's Romantic Fiction

The Letting Love In Series

- **His Heart's Burden** — (*books2read.com/ HisHeartsBurden*)
- **Her Guarded Heart** — (*books2read.com/ HerGuardedHeart*)
- **Her Heart's Desire** — (*books2read.com/ HerHeartsDesire*)
- **His Hearts Promise** — (*books2read.com/ HisHeartsPromise*)
- **Her Heart's Wish** — (*Coming Spring 2025*)
- **Her Heart's Secret** — (*Coming Spring 2025*)
- **Her Lonely Heart** — (*Coming Winter 2025*)
- **His Forgotten Heart** — (*Coming Winter 2025*)
- **Her Fighting Heart** — (*Coming Winter 2026*)
- **His Racing Heart** — (*Coming Winter 2026*)
- **Her Jaded Heart** — (*Coming Winter 2026*)

CONTEMPORARY ROMANCE

- **Windswept Whispers** — (*books2read.com/ WindsweptWhispers*)

HOLIDAY STORIES

- **Merry and Bright** — *(Coming Winter 2025)*

INTERNATIONAL COZY MYSTERIES

The Travel Visa Mysteries

- **Betrayal by the Bay** (Book 1) — *(Coming Spring 2025)*
- **Ended on Easter Island** (Book 2) — *(Coming Spring 2025)*
- **Suspense on the Serengeti** (Book 3) — *(Coming Spring 2025)*

ROMANTIC FANTASY

The Changeling Chronicles Trilogy

- **Beyond the Veil** (Book 1) — *(Coming Spring 2025)*
- **Whispers of the Fey** (Book 2) — *(Coming Spring 2025)*
- **The Feyborn Legacy** (Book 3) — *(Coming Spring 2025)*

Acknowledgments

Thank you to all of those in my corner. To my amazing beta readers, critique partners and editors, who are not only fantastic friends but also amazing authors in their own right:

Bonnie Phelps, Deb Julienne, Diane Wiggs.

Thank you Amanda Gale, Nellie Steel, Rhys Shaw, and Sherry Soule for always being there to bounce ideas off of.

To the Groundbreakers group, our Dragon's roar! Aliki, Angie, Patty, Monica, Joanna, and of course our amazing mentors, Scarlett Moss and Craig Huber.

About the Author

An insatiable reader of all genres since her childhood, Dawn is a globetrotter hungry to discover new places and experience unique adventures.

She can be found indulging in her husband's first love of summer camping in the mountains or luxuriating in the open seas while cruising to exotic destinations during the frigid winter months.

When she's not jet-setting she can be found in

Central Valley California with her family and their many rescue animals.

To read her blog, get the latest news, future release dates, or to join her ARC team sign up for her newsletter at *www.DawnBaca.com.*

Social Media

facebook.com/DawnMBaca

bsky.app/profile/BacaDawn

amazon.com/author/dawnbaca

bookbub.com/profile/dawn-baca

goodreads.com/dawnbaca

tiktok.com/@bacadawn

x.com/BacaDawn

youtube.com/DawnBaca

pinterest.com/dawnmbaca

instagram.com/dawnbaca

Paperback ISBN: 978-1-7329615-5-5
Cover: Rax Well
Editors: Amaya Dean & Helena Graves
Chapter Image: Greek Sea created in Canva

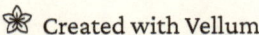 Created with Vellum